ACCIDENTS WILL HAPPEN

ANDREW J FIELD

HIT THE NORTH

Published by Hit the North
Mill Wharf
Tweedmouth
Berwick upon Tweed
Northumberland
TD15 2BP

First published in Great Britain 2025

Hardback: ISBN: 978-1-9191647-0-0

Paperback: ISBN: 978-1-9191647-1-7

A catalogue record for this book is available from the British Library.

ALSO BY ANDREW J FIELD

Without Rules
All Down the Line
After the Bridge

For Anthony, Janis & Pam

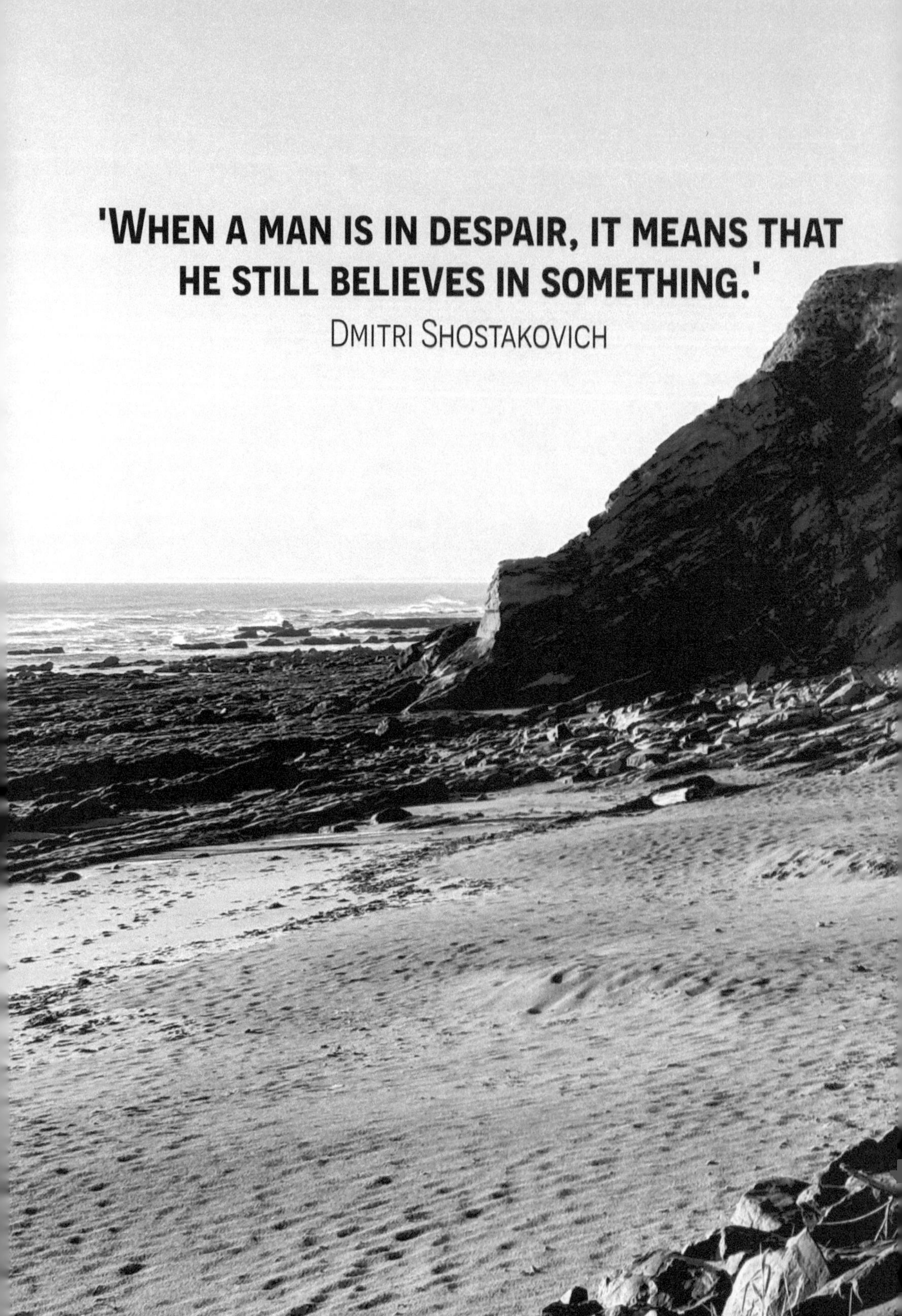

'WHEN A MAN IS IN DESPAIR, IT MEANS THAT HE STILL BELIEVES IN SOMETHING.'
DMITRI SHOSTAKOVICH

ON
THE
RECORD

1

Standing straight and tall, he solemnly, sincerely and truly declares and affirms the evidence he gives is the truth, the whole truth and nothing but the truth. His voice is as powerful as his muscular body, the left side of his bald head and face is disfigured by serious burn scars.

There are gasps from the public gallery behind him. People react with shock when they see him, but it is their problem, not his, so long as they keep their distance and don't sneak up unannounced.

He focuses on Harriet Cavendish sitting at the bench, looking down on him through bifocals. A smallish diamond-encrusted gold cross reveals a woman of expensive faith. He's wearing a black suit, white shirt and green 42 Commando silk tie dotted with white daggers.

She is the Northumberland coroner who will determine the circumstances behind Lisa Wright's death. She has allocated a day for the inquest. That's not a long time in his view, as he stands in the witness box, like a naughty schoolboy, waiting for her to address him.

He's been in a coroner's court before, giving evidence about mates dying too young in foreign lands and is used to authority's intimidating formality.

After a pause, Cavendish asks, for the record, for his full name, even though her office has been communicating with him since Lisa's death six months ago last autumn.

'Mike Nicholls.'

'Your profession, Mr Nicholls?'

He says he is a personal trainer who worked as a stunt man until a car accident left him a spitting image of Niki Lauda.

How silly am I with the flippant Lauda comment. Typical meathead masking my nervousness with dark comedy. Black humour is OK on a run ashore with the lads, but not for this lot. They don't understand our fatalism where survival in war is potluck. If a bullet or an IED has my name on it, there's nowt I can do about it, unless me and my mates retaliate first and eliminate a real or imagined threat, but that self-preservation is called a war crime, and they'll chase you for the rest of your natural born. Look at Ireland. Been happening all my life. Soldiers getting done while the politicians retire to the House of Lords. Good work if you can get it.

Cavendish says she hardly notices his injuries and asks him to continue. She's trying to be kind, but she winces when she sees his face.

He tells her prior to the movies he was a Royal Marine and served in Afghanistan and Iraq fighting for Queen and country. He joined at seventeen with his best mate, Charlie Cortez. They were the ginger twins, not that anyone can tell by his bald scarred head, missing eyebrows and half an ear.

Cavendish thanks him for his service and gets down to the nitty-gritty. The reason why they are here. She asks if he could tell the court how he knew Lisa Wright.

Mike explains he was her personal trainer for about six months. He was recommended by a friend who plays the trombone, a former professor of music in the Royal Marines based in Portsmouth. Lisa turned up on his doorstep and said she wanted to get fitter and faster.

I am tweaking the truth. I answered my front door thinking who is calling at this hour, and a bright light flashes in my face, half blinding me. I am too stunned to react and see dots in my eyes until I realise there is a young woman in blue jeans, white tee-shirt and black pumps beaming at me and lowering a Polaroid camera from her face. Nobody uses them anymore.

Her actual first words were, 'I am pissed, do you want to talk? I've been running round in circles, going nowhere fast, making myself dizzy. I am a woman overboard, in danger of drowning and somebody needs to throw me a rope. I need a personal trainer.'

'That's me?'

'That's you,' she replies, slurring.

'You're drunk.'

'I'll be sober when the morning comes. You're a pretty boy.'

'What about the scars?'

She laughs and hands me a polaroid picture of myself, caught by surprise on my own front doorstep. I've been well and truly ambushed.

'I see no scars. You got a loo? Let me in, I think I am going to be sick.'

She was.

All down the hall and over me and herself.

Carrots everywhere.

I know who she is. Been in the town a short while. Likes to party.

'Anyone I can call?'

'No, I am alone in the whole wild world.'

I help her undress and shower. She puts on Angelina's blue pyjamas and sleeps in the recovery position in my absent sister's bedroom. I stayed watching her all night in case she vomited again and choked to death.

When she woke up, she asked if I had raped her when she was unconscious. Was pleased I hadn't. She has a low opinion of people, starting with herself, shaking in the morning, full of self-hate and loathing while we drink coffee and eat cold porridge.

'I am sober now, still want to talk?'

'You want to get fitter and faster. Stop binge drinking for starters.'

'Let's write down our rules. I am liking you, Mike Nicholls. I am Lisa Wright until I am wrong.'

We make a pledge to cut down her drinking and get her fighting fit so she can chase the boys. As she suggested, we write it down on a piece of paper and we sign it. Pin it on the fridge. It's still there.

That story is not for sharing with this lot or anybody else.

'Could you tell me what happened the day Lisa died. You were the last person to see her alive.'

'Everything was cool. We'd done this run dozens of times. We were on an early morning training run from Berwick's old Bridge to Spittal promenade, up and over the cliffs, about-turning at the Scremerston level crossing and racing back the way we came. We reach the end of the promenade. Climb up an embankment with the new million quid George Craig glasshouses to the right and our path across the cliffs to our left...'

I pause, sip a cold glass of water and collect my thoughts. What happens next is frozen in my mind and I live with it daily; vivid memories crop up when I least expect them. Articulating my version of events out loud feels raw, and the emotions catch me by surprise. Like Lisa's Polaroid. And I can do nothing about it.

The coroner asks if he is OK.

Sure, he says, two fifty yards down the cliff path, he is conscious he can't hear her running. He glances over his shoulder, and she isn't there. If she's having a leak or injured, why not call out? He retraces his steps and looks over the edge of the cliffs, at the rocks and sea, just in case.

He pauses again, sips more water and takes a few deep breaths. This is much harder than he thought it was going to be.

'Take your time,' says Cavendish.

'I spot her body on the rocks. Doesn't look good. I basically go into automatic Marine mode. Act like I am in Basra after an IED attack, and we're surrounded by injured and dying people with bits of their bodies blown everywhere by the explosion. Crapping yourself won't help the wounded and maimed, calmness saves lives.'

Mike says he called 999 as an intercity train whistled by. He was conscious he was losing vital seconds, but it is better to be accurate than fast. He tells the inquest a young lad died here on the cliffs a few years back because the emergency operator misheard the kid's original call and almost everyone was looking for him on the north side of the estuary, not the southern side.

'The operator tells me to wait for the emergency services, but I don't want Lisa washing out to sea and her body lost. I quickly recon the cliffs looking for a place I can safely clamber down and reach her. I am no stranger to rocks and climbing up and down sheer cliffs is basic training for commandos. However, you've still got to work out a route and take your time, especially if no safety ropes are involved in the descent. A slip could be fatal.'

'Do you want five minutes?' asks the coroner.

'No, I make it to the bottom relatively quickly without too much difficulty and assess the situation. On the ground I see the damage to Lisa is catastrophic and there is nothing I can do except pick up a few pieces that had fallen off and hold her close to me until the RNLI and coastguard arrive, keep her company as her spirit drifts out to sea,' says Mike.

I'd sung the Stones' Wild Horses to her while I wait for the blue lights and a boat. The lines Jagger sings about suffering aching pains, no sweeping exits or offstage lines, feeling bitter and treating her unkind, ring so true as the winds blow away my words. I'd look soft and sentimental if I mention it to this lot and they'll laugh at me behind my back.

'Was she dead?'

'Yes?'

'Did you check her pulse? Check she was breathing.'

'No.'

'Why not?'

'I've seen dead people before. I know what they look like. That's why I lifted and held her. If she was alive, she might have broken her back and been paralysed if I moved her.'

'Thank you,' says Cavendish.

There is another pause while the coroner checks her notes, the slight delay allowing her to digest Mike's testimony and prepare for a new line of questioning.

'What was the weather like on the run?'

'Cold and very windy, very Berwick.'

'No sea fret making visibility poor.'

'No, no coastal fog. It wasn't warm enough.'

'You could see Holy Island clearly or Bamburgh Castle?'

'Not that I noticed. You get used to your surroundings.'

'Was it safe in your view?'

'Of course, I don't do reckless,' says Mike, aware his burn scars indicate the opposite. 'People walk, cycle and drive across the cliffs throughout the year, whether it is wet or dry. Ice is the killer. Lisa and I did that route dozens of times. It's fun and rugged.'

'No risks at all?'

'Cramp. Pulled muscles. Not catastrophic falls.'

'How or why do you think she fell?'

'I cannot speculate. One second she's there, next she's gone.'

'Could she have tripped or slipped and fallen over?'

'Yes. Anything could have happened. She was behind me and wasn't hanging on my right shoulder ready to overtake.'

'Could she have deliberately jumped?'

'Yes, but I didn't see her go over, and I am sorry, but I am not qualified to comment on Lisa's mental health. I am a former water soldier, a stunt man, not a psychiatrist, I don't have a crystal ball.'

'Saying you don't know is fine. We only want the facts if the possibility of suicide is one of the primary causes of her unnatural death.'

He says he understands but simply doesn't know. The emergency services muddied the area where she fell with their ambulances and police cars, so it was almost impossible to say yes or no to any signs of skid marks on the path. There are a couple of snickers from behind and he realises he should have said 'slip'.

Cavendish pauses and considers her notes carefully. Has he run the cliff route since the accident?

'Yes, two or three times a week.'

'Who with?'

'Just myself.'

'Why?'

'Nobody wants to come with me,' he deadpans, his thinly veiled sarcasm fooling nobody. He hears a derisive snort and a few gasps behind him in response to his unwarranted belligerence.

Cavendish blushes slightly, probably to hide her annoyance at his lack of respect to her and the crown, thinks Mike.

She pauses again and considers her next question.

'How well did you know Lisa?'

The question is delivered straight, but the coroner cannot mask her perception that all working-class men are goats chasing casual sex.

He tells her they socialised occasionally, drinking real ale in the Barrels and the Curfew, eating curries at Amran's on Hyde Hill, and having coffees and sausage baps in Northern Edge after a run.

'Did you notice her mood change in the days before her death?'

'No,' he lies.

Although I have just promised to tell the court the truth, I also vowed to Lisa that what was said in her bedroom stayed in her bedroom. I respect her privacy. It's the only thing she has left, apart from a few possessions stored in my house overlooking the Tweed estuary, the lighthouse at the end of the pier, and the Elizabethan walls protecting the town from rampaging Scots but not annoying tourists. They are locked away in my sister's cupboard. I collected them from John Armstrong's flat in Mount Street after the cops had a quick butchers. Three backpacks, two viola cases and her trusty Polaroid camera.

'Did you know she was taking antidepressants?'

'No,' he lies again, without any hesitation, proof he is a trustworthy witness. 'Lisa told me she missed playing music professionally, but she saw the pause in her career as a chance to recharge her batteries and find new playing avenues.'

'Did you and Lisa ever discuss sex abuse, generally or specifically?'

'No,' he lies for the third time, like Peter thrice denying Jesus at the last supper before the Romans crucified him. 'Why would we? Nothing to joke about, is it? No cheap laughs or thrills chatting about kiddy fiddlers.'

'Sorry, talking about the prospect of suicide is never easy for family and friends,' says Cavendish, 'And I appreciate your candour, if not your use of language.'

'They are words people use down the pub,' says Mike.

He swivels in the witness box and momentarily faces the dozen or so friends of Lisa Wright. All but four are female. All approximately her age in their late twenties, early thirties, apart from an older couple with large wooden crosses hanging around their necks and two middle-aged gents. They are all staring at him, like he's a circus clown about to perform magic tricks at a child's birthday party.

Their eyes are magnetically drawn to his scars. Only Lisa's GP and the WPC working in Berwick aren't shocked. They are used to the damage done. He knows them both. Berwick is a small town. Everybody knows everybody. What happens in the town, stays in the town, like the bedroom and the pub. Outsiders are tolerated, never warmly welcomed. Longevity does not make a resident an insider. Trust does. Actions do. Words mean nothing in isolation.

'I am very sorry for your loss, she fell on my watch, under my care and I'd do anything to turn back the clock. Pick a different route. I feel responsible, almost guilty.'

There is a pause after he speaks and he can hear the ticking of the court clock above the coroner's desk. Soon it will be over. All the interested parties and persons have already seen his statement and he's not deviated from it, despite his intentions to partly tell the actual truth when he drove down from Berwick.

'Thank you for your testimony today and your courage. Before you step down, we have a couple of questions from interested parties.'

There is another longer pause, while Mike waits for a question.

'My name is Callum John Petty, and this is my wife, Susan Petty. We're Lisa's parents and we'd like to say a big thank you to Mr Nicholls for his efforts to save our daughter, and we forgive him for any involvement in Lisa's death. The Lord works in mysterious ways. Maybe he wants Lisa by his side and can't wait.'

'Thank you,' says Mike, resisting the urge to belittle Petty's interventionist God for taking Lisa too soon.

'Is that all?' asks the coroner. 'No specific question about the events of the day?'

'No questions as such. We just want to let Michael know he has the Lord's — and our — forgiveness. We encourage you to all embrace God and take the pledge with the Brotherhood of Jesus and start your journey to eternal redemption.'

'Thank you. Next,' says Cavendish. 'Your name for the record?'

'Sally Palmer. I was Lisa's best friend. I am surprised at your testimony. Are you saying she never talked to you about sexual abuse, despite all the time you spent together?'

'No,' says Mike. 'She never did.'

'Are you sure?'

'I think I'd have remembered if she had,' Mike says, turning and looking at Sally Palmer, flowery dress, dishevelled red hair pinned up and a pale freckly face.

'She never confided in you at all?'

'No.'

'You were her closest friend in Berwick for six months?'

'We ran and trained together. That's all, doesn't make us man and wife. There's a twenty-year age difference if you're suggesting we might have been better friends,' says Mike. 'I am sure she had lots of male friends her own age, even in Berwick, where we're overstocked with retirees and pensioners.'

'Less of the witty asides, not the right place, Mr Nicholls,' admonishes Cavendish.

'But you knew her well?' asks Sally.

'Not enough to be listed as an interested person for this inquest.'

'You're not the only one excluded as an IP,' says Sally. 'Did she have a nickname for you? Did she sleep over at yours?'

'Lots of people sleep over at mine, crash out after a few too many wets.'

'Is this relevant?' asks Cavendish.

'She gave her best friends nicknames. I was Nicole, after the Aussie actress, Nicole Kidman. She was Angel, because her viola playing was heavenly — and she looked like one.'

'I've met Nicole through Tom, a couple of times. Lisa's name for me was Pretty Boy,' says Mike, thinking he could see a slight resemblance between the two women, although Sally was plainer, less charismatic.

'What did you call her?'

'Occasionally, Stitch,' says Mike. 'She got it bad on her first run. I pushed her too hard. Mostly Lisa.'

'Why?'

'That's her name.'

'No more questions.'

There is another pause before a second male voice pipes up. He introduces himself as Rupert Burr, a solicitor representing Ms Kaitlin Becker, the head administrator of Newcastle's Great Northern Philharmonic Orchestra.

'Mr Nicholls, can I confirm you have just said it was an accident and had nothing to do with suicide?'

'No,' says Mike, turning to face the diminutive balding lawyer who looks like he is sitting down even though he is standing. 'I saw nothing. She was behind me. And I am not a mind reader, so I don't know what she was thinking.'

'Thank you,' says Burr.

'No more questions? Thank you for your time,' says Cavendish, 'would you mind staying on Mr Nicholls, I might want to recall you later this afternoon before we close.'

'Why?'

'I might have some more questions,' she replies.

He thought he would be allowed to go home. A forty-five-minute drive from the coroner's court in Morpeth back up the A1 to Berwick for a beer in the Curfew to toast Lisa's spirit, wherever it roams. He has done his bit and it was up to the inquest to decide how and why she died, not him.

Can the coroner make him stay? Will he be in contempt? Worse, will he be newsworthy? Life's easier slipping under the radar, being anonymous.

I've done my duty. Kept my promise to Lisa. Not mentioned the sexual abuse she said took place at the music college. Nor have I explained how and why I think a shite erotic exploitation thriller written by a J.D. Hammerhead was the cause of her sudden demise. That was going to be my revised story, until I changed my mind the second I stepped into the witness box and knew I could not let Lisa down yet again, not when it is obvious nobody really cared about her. We had made a pledge in writing, signed it in red ink like it was our blood. A promise must mean something otherwise what are we doing here?

Now, I just want to go home and let sleeping dogs lie, forget about her pale blue eyes and her sparkling mirror-ball smile. She deserves better, but white knights in shining armour cannot save people who would rather die than live. So far, I've successfully contained my anger in the most trying circumstances, like I did in the immediate aftermath of my almost fatal death-drive in the United States of Accidents, before somebody convinced me the time was ripe to be unlucky in Kentucky. I know I must let it go, no matter how much my blood boils. But saying that is far easier said than actually doing it. Not when I've got Charlie Cortez bending what's left of my left ear, whispering why should anyone who contributed to Lisa's death get a free ride while my conscience is perpetually under attack. Good old Charlie, used the same rationale after my own horrific car crash on a mismanaged film set in California. Who wins, Charlie or my conscience? It's a constant battle, like an alcoholic staring at a bottle of gin, tonic water, and a tall glass full of ice and two slices of lemon. Just a matter of time, unless the soak has the strength to leave the room and remove temptation. Not many do. Takes a big man to admit he's wrong and an even bigger man to walk away.

2

Mike Nicholls exits the witness box, eyes straight ahead, and sits at the rear of the courtroom, back against the wall. He scans the public gallery, always anticipating the worst, more out of habit than necessity. Although this is England and not Iraq or Afghanistan, he doesn't like people creeping around unseen behind him. Most Royal Marines share the same nervousness; a few are worse, like Charlie Cortez, hiding away from civilisation for his own sanity.

The coroner and her team are prepping themselves to welcome the next witness.

The religious parents of Lisa Wright are nearest the bench, huddled together like conjoined twins. Two female uniformed police officers chat like they are on a riverside picnic, better than walking the beat. The short lawyer and his client look unreasonably nervous when they are not even on trial; nobody is, apart from Lisa's reputation.

Mike recognises Lisa's GP — Helen Bishop — from Berwick. She is sat with her human resources rep from her practice, Molly James. He briefly said hello to them earlier when he first arrived.

Three girlfriends of Lisa Wright are several seats away in the back row, faces red and blotchy, advertising their grief. One bloke, dressed like a country squire, toys with a newspaper crossword, another is scribbling shorthand in a notebook. Mike will have a chat with the reporter next break, explain about respecting the dead, and keeping his name out of any scoop the journalist is planning to publish.

The coroner invites Sally Palmer into the witness box.

The tall ginger woman in a flowery dress takes the bible in her hand and swears by Almighty God the evidence she shall give shall be the truth, the whole truth, and nothing but the truth.

Mike's not impressed by her act. Unlike him, she's a believer. And unlike him, she's totally, rather than partially, responsible for Lisa's death, as the inquest is about to find out.

Cavendish reads the rape identification riot act.

Before Ms Palmer starts her testimony, I must inform you all, it is a criminal offence under the Sexual Offences (Amendment) Act 1992 to publish or broadcast any matter that is likely to identify an alleged victim of a sexual offence. I am therefore reminding everyone that there must be no publication of any details that are likely to lead members of the public to identify any person whose name has been mentioned in this court as a victim of such an offence.

After a beat or two to allow the gravity of her words to sink in, Cavendish asks for her name for the court record.

'Sally Palmer.'

'Your profession?'

Sally says she's an A&E staff nurse at Newcastle's general hospital, and volunteers at the North of Tyne rape crisis centre. Once a week, every Thursday. She sees rape and abuse victims coming into A&E all the time. Breaks her heart, but she stays professional and detached. A&E staff collect evidence from victims' bodies, patch them up and send them home with a leaflet. They have no option but to forget about them and wait for the next ruined life on the assault conveyor belt. She compensates by volunteering at the crisis centre, helps them the best way she can to try and repair the damage, even if it puts a strain on her relationship with her husband, Ian Palmer.

The coroner thanks her and asks how she knows Lisa Wright.

Sallys says they were best friends at the Great Northern College of Music and Performing Arts. Lisa was a far better musician, more suited to observing a punishing practising regime than Sally ever was. Senior school staff gave Lisa preferential treatment including extra private tuition. Despite all the praise and their different abilities, their friendship was rock solid, maybe because they were both lanky stick insects without middle-class safety nets. When they were auditioning, Lisa was more concerned about Sally than herself.

Sally hesitates and, like Mike earlier, reaches for a glass of water. Like him, he imagines she's finding talking about her best friend in a formal court more difficult than she anticipated.

'Are you OK to go on?'

'Sure. We were angels with dirty faces, blank minds and long legs, good time girls not taking ourselves too seriously,' says Sally, almost whispering her words like she is reciting a poem.

I am feeling confused. I am not sure if Sally Palmer is a good actress or the real deal and I am just a mug falling for another distressed pretty face and long legs.

Her wavering voice and body language shows she's suffering, unlike the psychos I've lived and worked with in war zones, celebrating brutal killing sprees with beers and karaoke machines slaughtering singalong tunes like Meat Loaf's Bat out of Hell and Neil Diamond's Sweet Caroline. Charlie Cortez sang a mean version of John Lennon and Yoko Ono's Instant Karma, everyone shining on with the moon and the stars and the sun, but karma's still gonna get ya, sooner or later.

He was big on karma, was Charlie. So am I, to be fair. justice is for rich people to buy whenever they want. Just a matter of negotiating the right price.

Sally explains Lisa successfully auditioned for the Great Northern Philharmonic Orchestra while she started a nursing career and played music for fun as an amateur.

They'd gone out on the razz and chatted about Lisa touring Japan and America and Sally's life-saving gruesome hospitals stories — one surgeon stitched a massive hole in a heart after a stabbing. If that surgeon hadn't been on call, the dude would have bled to death. The consultant was like a classical musician, the way he worked.

Lisa loved Sally's real-life stories.

'Can you stick to the facts, please,' says the coroner.

'I am digressing, sorry. Lisa always said her success has an expensive price tag, but I thought she was being self-deprecating to be kind to me because she was going places, and I wasn't. And then...then...then...'

'Can you speak closer to the microphone, please,' says Cavendish, leaning forward to indicate to her whispering witness that she is struggling to hear her. 'It is difficult to transcribe your testimony if your voice isn't loud enough.'

'Sorry.'

There is a short delay. Sally is looking less composed in the witness box, fidgeting with her hands, unable to decide what to do with them.

'Your friendship?'

'Our friendship was about to change after a sexual assault.'

Sally pauses her testimony. Mike sees her exposed neck redden. The courtroom dynamic changes. Cavendish leans forward, a heron fishing on a riverbank waiting patiently to catch a fresh fish supper. The reporter licks his lips and the tip of his pencil lasciviously. The other man stops toying with his crossword puzzle. The two female police grimace. They've heard similar stuff before many times. The girlfriends of Lisa Wright are all ears. They cannot help themselves watching the soap opera unfold, their tears and smudged mascara forgotten.

'We were out in a club in Newcastle, a girly weekend, staying in the Malmaison on the quayside, shopping during the day, dancing at night. We met two lads, I'll call them Ben and Colin, but that's not their real names. Mature university students with Village People moustaches, tight blue jeans and loose vests showing off gym-bunny bodies.

'Naturally, we thought they were gay, and we pretend we were a lesbian couple too for a laugh. After the nightclub shuts, we carry on partying at our waterfront hotel.

'Fast forward half an hour, I am semi-conscious, clearly not capable of consenting, slumped on a sofa, half watching Angel and Ben dancing badly to music videos on the telly. Colin is next to me, stroking my arms, shoulders and hair, unzipping the front of my little black dress, whispering two is company, three is a crowd and four is an orgy. I tell him to stop messing with me several times, trying to push him away, but he ignores me, his fingers outside my bra, inside my bra, pulling my bra up, outside my black tights, inside my black tights, pulling them down, and then, then, then, inside me. That's not being too graphic, being finger fuc...'

Sally's struggling. She stops herself completing the sentence, although her anger is all too obvious. She needs to be calmer, or the courtroom will think she is neurotic. Charlie Cortez would call her a cat strangler, a pre-menopausal bride going home and killing the thing she loves most. Charlie's vicious, like his namesake, the murderous conquistador, Hernán Cortés, who conquered Mexico. Victory came at the expense of an Aztec ruler Montezuma II, who died fighting Spanish forces. Neil Young wrote about the illegal invasion, a lingering wailing blues about a civilisation doomed regardless of its serenity. Like love. No matter how deep or serious. Like Lisa.

'Will this help us understand if Lisa took her own life?' asks Cavendish.

'Am I being too graphic? Shall I be more sanitised, less explicit?'

The words are delivered like machine gun fire, rapid and fast.

'I know emotions are running high, Ms Palmer, but remember where you are and who you are addressing. I represent the crown. Your testimony feels very overwhelming, and you have the right to freely express yourself. However, can we try and stick to the facts, your testimony must stay relevant and not be so, so graphic.'

'Yes. But it is crucial you know my sexual assault was the only reason Lisa told me she was the victim of sustained abuse over many years, not just one night. She was empathising with me, reacting to Colin asking if I like to be choked when I come, his fingers still inside me. Lisa's watching the other lad unzipping and exposing himself. If I don't tell you that, you'll not understand Lisa's response to their terrifying behaviour.'

'I understand where you are coming from Ms Palmer, continue.'

'Lisa yells at them to fuck right off or she'll scream FIRE and wake up the entire hotel. Her voice is so convincing they stop messing with me and turn aggressively to face her. They are bigger and more powerful than us and will swat us away like flies. Lisa smashes an empty wine bottle on a dressing table and waves the corkscrew and the jagged glass at them, a blond Boudicca, red lips and mascara running down her face, threatening to gouge their eyes out and cut them to fuck so even their mums won't recognise them.'

Sally stops to get a second wind. She sips water. Breathes slowly to calm herself. Shakes in the witness box.

'I am very sorry this happened to you, and I know you're angry, but again, how is your assault relevant to this inquest?' asks Cavendish. 'Can we stay focused on the facts, please?'

'I am coming to it, be patient, please. I was devastated by what had happened. Nobody's ever taken advantage of me when I am drunk and high. But Lisa's not devastated one iota, despite her very convincing violent outburst. She, she's...unperturbed by my sexual assault or the prospect of us getting raped by animals.'

I can feel myself clenching my fists in anger and hope I can hide my emotions. James, my old man back home in Berwick, taught me early doors to respect women before I could even walk. My mum, my sister Angelina, in fact, all the fairer sex, my dad's words, not mine. Jimmy was a hard man who had standards. He was a foot soldier with a good eye for a shot. An infantryman who sniped. A proud guardsman. He was with the Scots Guards in Northern Ireland when they cleared "no-go areas" in Derry and the Bogside. Same time as the Paras lost control of their discipline on Sunday Bloody Sunday. He tells me he lost three mates and gained a son, although he missed my birth. He would tell me the bastards who hurt women and girls should be hammered on their heads like a pile-driver until they were battered senseless.

I keep my face neutral. Restraint, observation, and selective use of extreme violence were the lessons my old man had taught me, but he didn't have access to my best mate. Calling Charlie Cortez, we need your galleons and your guns. Or, to be more accurate, your standard issue SA80 A2 rifle firing, or the L96 .338 sniper rifle you used to eliminate distant targets, your ever-reliable Fairbairn Sykes commando double-edged knife never far away for silent close-up kills. I cannot imagine Charlie showing the same patience as me at an inquest. He was — or is — a man of action, not words. Cortez says the more men talk, the less they want to act until they freeze into inertia.

'Thankfully, the two lads want to avoid a bloodbath and back off, grabbing their things and throwing insults at us as they leave. Lisa slams the door behind, and I say give me a few minutes before we call the police and report them. She says that is the last thing we are going to do. The police will never believe us. The cops, the CPS and rich boys' lawyers will hang us out to dry. Once we are identified as assault victims, we are damaged goods. She said I'd no longer be seen as a nurse, but a cock teaser toying with nice boys from nice families. Same will be true for her. Whenever she plays, the audience will be chatting about her from behind their concert programmes and wrinkled bejewelled hands, suggesting that there is never smoke without fire, especially if the slutty violist was a sexually complicit teenager who happily broke the law and never told anyone because she was living the life.

'I counter that the police and the courts will treat us with respect, and she says get real. Those two suited-and-booted wannabe rapists will swear on their mothers' lives we were gagging for group sex. Their expensive lawyers will point to lewd videos of us necking each other, your short zippy black plastic dress fitting like a second skin, sexy matching black bra and pants, six-inch stiletto heels. Come on, Sally, grow up, what chance do we have?'

Lisa is right again. Lawyers, and Marine officers and movie producers, will fuck you over with their posh words delivered with sniper Jimmy's devastating accuracy. Most are bullies and pull their metaphorical punches when facing genuine hard men or nut jobs. Men like me and Charlie Cortez. The first thing we learned in the Marines was how to kill a man with our bare hands. Great for staying alive, but knowing how to stop a man stone dead in seconds is a negative on a CV once state-trained assassins leave the services.

'I was shocked at her attitude and asked her how she knows all this. She says, because she had been abused many times and silence is a better option than eternal humiliation and ridicule. Despite appearances, she is not brave like me, she doesn't want to fight the world, she just wants to be left alone to play music and get on with her life.'

Sally Palmer pauses and drinks even more water. Mike tries to judge the mood in the room. Are the people at the inquest more sympathetic towards Sally after her very personal revelations.

'How long ago was this?'

'Three and a half years ago,' says Sally, and gives the court the exact dates and times that are already in her written statement.

'And did Lisa talk about her own humiliation?' asks Cavendish. 'Did she give you real details that we can check? Is this the point of your extended monologue?'

'Yes, I am finally coming to it, but you have to have the whole picture, not a few small jigsaw pieces.'

'I understand.'

'She swore me to absolute secrecy, said she would deny she ever said anything if I told anyone. Made me sign a piece a paper. She kept it after I signed. I don't know what happened to it before you ask.'

I cannot help myself nodding in agreement. Lisa said similar words to me when I found her with the rope and the book. Another one of her pledges. I am surprised at the apparent antagonism that's developed between the witness and the coroner. That's not how an inquest should be run. This should have been discussed, agreed and disclosed pre-inquest rather than them having a public tiff. Falling out in public is sloppy. Maybe Sally's strayed from her agreed script? Then again, I've been disingenuous by omitting the book from my written statement submitted months ago and my verbal testimony delivered today. Difference was I am calm in the box; she is agitated and antsy, bristling with belligerence. But I am older and wiser and know how to play the game. It is the least Lisa deserves, because she never got a second chance.

'What did she tell you?' asks Cavendish. 'And when?'

'An hour after my assault. She confessed she was having a triangular affair that was probably illegal and involved multiple sex crimes. She said the physical relationship started when she was fourteen and she was in their study having extra tuition. She said the first time the wife lifted her skirt, took her pants off and went down on her she froze. The husband started masturbating. After, they had said well-done, like she'd just put down a seven-letter word on a scrabble board.'

There is pause while Sally sips her water. Mike notices everyone's listening intently, faces full of disapproval, but still rapt. He sympathises with Sally. Graphic sexual descriptions are OK for Gillian Anderson's *Want* book rammed from pink cover to pink cover with explicit female fantasies, but not for an inquest.

'You OK to continue, Ms Palmer?'

Sally says yes, she couldn't believe what she was hearing. How many times. Lisa says she lost count, two or three times a week, her special tuition time.

'Why? I asked her. She laughs and cries at the same time, the tears automatic, even though her face still looks calm and collected. Her abusers told Lisa she was special, the beautiful one, a tall girl with the innocence of a schoolgirl blessed with big tits. They said they loved Lisa as their own and their support was important for her musical ambitions. I told her they groomed and exploited her, she was still a child, no matter how well stacked upstairs. She says she got to play for the Great Northern Philharmonic and travelled the world at somebody else's expense, so all her young dreams did come true.

'I asked her why she didn't tell them to stop like we did with the two rapists. Or tell someone. The police. A social worker. A doctor. A nurse. Another teacher. Her parents. Me, her best friend. She says she wasn't going to ruin her musical career because of sex. Not when they said she would be expelled from the college for taking drugs and stealing and drinking.

'I told her that they were blackmailing her and that only made their crimes even worse. She says she did take drugs and drink with them, and they gave her pocket money as thank you presents when they finished playing on her body like she was a rag doll.

'It was a sick question, but I asked her what they did to her. She said often the wife would perform cunnilingus, wearing Lisa like a horse's feedbag, one finger up her bum. Like the first time, her viola teacher would watch. Betty would hurt her, strangle her, spank her, insert objects. She didn't realise her accidental slip of the tongue. She had just identified Bryan Bray and his wife Betty to me. The other viola teachers were single white females. Only one couple were a husband-and-wife team. Betty was just as visible as Bryan in her student safeguarding role, an irony if there ever was one.

'I asked Lisa how did she cope? Lisa says she surrendered to the pain and thought of a musical score such as Dmitri Shostakovich's *Symphony No. 5*. She played it in her head while they played with her.'

You know Lisa has played me the symphony in my house numerous times. She would come and practice here as her housemates would complain about the noise. I liked her playing, although I knew nothing about classical music. I was into rock and country and the blues like Cash and The Clash, the Redskins, Dexys, Bruce, Prine and Kris, Neil, Skynyrd and the Truckers, Nick Cave, PJ and the Monkeys. She said the Russian composer Shostakovich had to appease a dictator and lectured me passionately about how the composer cleverly employed a powerful and expressive musical language, blending traditional symphonic forms with modern harmonic and melodic ideas. His blending contrasting textures, dynamic shifts, and recurring motifs were beyond Stalin's comprehension. I remember nodding and taking her word for it, glad she loved at least one part of her life. She was the expert on classical affairs. Both her violas are still at my house, locked in a cupboard. They must be worth a few quid if she was a professional musician. Nobody has ever asked me for them back. Or the rest of her kit I collected from John Armstrong the day after she died. He wanted to relet the flat before Lisa's body was cold, mercenary cunt. I left my contact details with him, but I never heard anything. None of her family has contacted me to tell me when her funeral was taking place, so I never went to say goodbye and I didn't want to intrude on their grief if I was responsible for her death. Maybe I can chat to the Pettys today, clear the air.

'I asked her how long it went on for and she said four years, but that it is history, and it does not matter anymore. That part of her life is a big black box with the lid nailed shut. No point opening it and releasing bad memories. I asked her when it ended and she said graduation day, they had lost interest in her. She was too old, and she laughs. I was wondering to myself how can she be so ice cold and callous? This is my best friend, except I don't recognise her anymore.

'Finally, I asked her outright, was it Bryan and Betty Bray? She said she was not going to tell me because we were never going to talk about this again. She said she was telling me because of our close shave with Ben and Colin. I had to understand that I had to suck it up and bury it deep inside me. See, I told you, I'd get there in the end,' says Sally.

'And how did you react?' asks Cavendish.

'I said she needed help and if she could not open-up to me, she should speak to a professional counsellor who would respect client confidentiality. I gave her the card of Simon Lord and said he offers a couple of pro bono hours each week at the rape crisis centre. I always keep a few cards on me. Our clients said he was good. She asked me again to swear blind to never tell anyone because she could not live her life with the shame. I asked if the Brays sexually assaulted other kids. They hadn't assaulted me but what about our prettier peers, the girlfriends of Lisa Wright behind me.

'Lisa said she was the only one. They only loved her. That was her confession. An hour's conversation in a hotel in Newcastle at 4am. Can I sit down? I am exhausted and feel sick.'

Sally sits down and huffs and puffs a couple of times, sounding like the dolphins when they visit the Tweed estuary for fresh mackerel suppers.

A couple of minutes later, she stands up again.

'Thank you, Ms Palmer, your openness is appreciated and understood. What happened next?' asks Cavendish.

'The next day I report my assault, and I report what Lisa had said, suggesting it was more than likely the Brays by a process of elimination. They were the only ones who ticked all the boxes.'

'You'd agreed not to, signed a piece of paper.'

'That was under duress. In the heat of the moment my signature meant nothing.'

'Why didn't you let Lisa decide when to talk to the police?'

'She was living in denial, and I had to make sure other kids were safe. Might have taken months or years for Lisa to speak out. How many others would suffer in the interim? One child on my conscience is one too many.'

'And did Lisa find out you had spoken to the police?'

'Yes.'

'How?'

'She asked straight after the police first interviewed her if I had grassed her up and I said yes. She told me I'd betrayed her. She could never trust me. Now her life would be hell. And she'd never forgive me. She should have let Ben and Colin rape me so I would know what it felt like. See if I was so keen to jump in front of a judgmental train. If I withdrew my statement, we could be best friends again.'

'Why didn't you do as she asked?'

'My silence would make me complicit. Equally as guilty as the Brays. I couldn't have that on my conscience.'

'Did you explain that to Lisa?'

'No. We never saw each other again in person, although we spoke on the phone and texted for a bit while she tried to make me withdraw my statement. I was in a Catch-22 situation. If the Brays abused other children and teenagers, I would never have been able to forgive myself. I contacted both the college and the orchestra anonymously on behalf of the rape crisis centre, and said we had allegations from a sex abuse client mentioning the Brays by name.'

'What happened?'

'With what?'

'Your own assault and the letters you sent out?'

'Is it relevant?'

'No, I suppose not.'

'No response to the letters.'

'Thank you for your testimony.'

'If push came to shove, I'd do the same all over again,' says Sally.

'One final question, did Lisa and you ever discuss suicide?'

'Yes.'

'As I said earlier, she said she could not live with the humiliation, she would rather be dead.'

'You never thought about withdrawing it?'

'No. I knew Simon Lord was counselling her about the abuse, as he'll explain later. And then six months later there was no need. The Brays were killed in a road traffic accident while on holiday in Portugal, or was it Italy or Spain. Somewhere in Europe. Car crash or a coach. There was no one to prosecute.'

'Thank you for your time. We have some questions from family and friends and colleagues.'

Poetic justice. Karma. Instant karma. I searched online as soon as Lisa gave me their names to find out what Bryan and Betty Bray were doing now and where they hid out. Me and Charlie would pay them a midnight visit, except a terrifying road with incredible zigzag turns located in the Italian Alps saved us the trouble.

From the newspaper coverage online about the UK inquest that followed their deaths in Europe, the Brays were models of the establishment, pillars of society. They went to same-sex public schools before meeting at music college in Manchester and marrying at Cambridge before becoming influential music teachers and critics. They had spent the last two decades in senior teaching and administrative roles at the Great Northern College of Music and Performing Arts.

They looked like any other happy affluent middle-aged couple who liked to travel the world in comfort. There were pictures online of them in Rome, New York, Barcelona, Paris, Sydney, Moscow, the Swiss Alps, the Grand Canyon, Bora Bora, Peru's Machu Picchu, Maui in Hawaii, the Maldives, Tanzania and Mount Kilimanjaro.

They were good looking, white crowned teeth, clear tanned skins and toned bodies. They were not identikit paedophiles and sex abusers. Then again, what does one look like? Not everyone dresses like Jimmy Savile or Gary Glitter. Some wear suits, elevator boots and rounded John Lennon spectacles.

Predictably, the Pettys repeat their forgiveness pitch.

'Sally's a good girl,' says Callum Petty. 'We'll say prayers, so God helps her on the righteous path until her rebirth.'

Rupert Burr, the lawyer for the head of admin for the Northern Philharmonic Orchestra, says there is no evidence any letter was sent to his client from a rape crisis centre.

'I posted the letter myself,' says Sally.

'So, you say. And you're the only person who alleges this abuse took place. Lisa's good friend Mike Nicholls said they never discussed it,' says Burr.

'I am just telling you what happened. That's all.'

'Were you jealous of the attention she got from the Brays because of her talent?'

'That's not relevant,' says Sally Palmer.

'Agreed, you should know better, Mr Burr.'

'I withdraw the question.'

'Good man,' says Cavendish.

I understand her question better now I have more context. She needs somebody to corroborate her story, otherwise she is a lone wolf howling at the moon, a neurotic cat strangler put down that men like Charlie Cortez apply to any woman who contradicts them. I am developing a habit of letting women down, first Lisa, now Sally.

Finally, a girlfriend of Lisa Wright, flautist Claudia Popp asks Sally Palmer why the portrait she paints of Lisa Wright is so different from their own personal memories?

'Maybe your relations were only skin deep? Not for me to comment.'

Cavendish tells them to stick to asking questions about facts and says it is a suitable time for a mid-morning break. Afterwards, they will hear from the police and Lisa's GP, and, after lunch, two more witnesses.

I stare into the middle distance and know my mission has been a success. An accidental conclusion is a formality and whoever contributed to her death is going to go unpunished, including the person feeding Angel Face stories to J.D. Hammerhead. I should be happy Lisa's death won't be suicide, but I still feel dirty, in need of a thorough rinse to spring clean my soul. And I am not the only one who stinks of filth.

3

The court automatically stands as one when the coroner leaves by a side door marked private, staff only. The girlfriends of Lisa Wright are first out. The Pettys, the police, the crossword professor, the doctor duo and the music admin boss and her short lawyer follow, no doubt keen for a breath of fresh air after the testimony they've endured. Only Sally Palmer and the journalist remain in the room messing with their things.

Sally glances over at Mike, makes eye contact and breaks it. She looks stunned, red-faced and sweaty. Mike could release her from her misery by confirming her story, but Sally Palmer is not his problem.

She's delving into her handbag and pulling out a Marlboro Red packet and a gold zip lighter. She has one last glance in his direction and leaves the courtroom, placing a cigarette in her mouth. The tab in her mouth seems to boost her self-esteem. She doesn't look quite so shell-shocked.

Mike watches the journalist pack his leather shoulder bag, slinging the strap over his shoulder. Slowly he walks towards the exit, diverting to the toilet. Mike follows him. It's empty. They stand at the urinals and then at the sink washing their hands.

'Who do you work for? Which paper?'

'A press agency in Newcastle.'

'Do they pay you well?'

'A basic fee and commission on syndication.'

'Will this sell?'

'A pretty girl being munched like a horse feedbag with a finger up her bum, like she's a glove puppet. I'll make a few extra quid, I expect.'

'You won't be able to report that,' says Mike. 'The witness is an assault victim. I'll give you two hundred notes, and you can go home and put your feet up.'

'Why would you do that?'

'They are going to say it's an accidental death. Lisa was never suicidal.'

'How do you know?'

They both stop washing their hands and shake them jazz style under the hand driers.

'Lisa was a good friend of mine. Besides, I am sensitive about my scars.'

'No, you're not. They're scary hard man souvenirs, if you're not used to seeing guilty tough guys in courts crumble when they are sentenced. But I'll give you the benefit of the doubt and take your money.'

'Good,' says Mike, and reaches into his suit trouser pocket. He pulls out a wedge and peels off four fifties and hands them to the reporter. 'Give me your number. I'll call you with the conclusion. No pictures and no mention of my name or my scars in your story.'

'Editing my words costs more,' says the journalist.

'Don't push your luck, quit while you're still standing,' says Mike, and opens the door to let the reporter leave.

Alone, he starts to wash his scarred hands gain, feeling grubby after bribing a weak journalist.

Somebody touches his shoulder. Instinctively, he raises his left elbow in line with his shoulders and drives it back, feeling his elbow hit softer gristle, pirouetting in one seamless movement.

'Jesus Christ.'

He's just smashed Callum Petty on the bridge of his nose. Lisa's father staggers like an unconscious boxer who is still managing to stand.

'I am so sorry mate. You sneaked up on me,' says Mike, inspecting the superficial damage. Fortunately, he never caught him flush, or he would be in trouble.

Callum Petty is looking at the blood streaming from his nose and Mike has a hand around his shoulder, guiding him to the wash basin and grabbing paper tissues with the other.

'Lean back and pinch the top of your nose for a few minutes. That will stop the bleeding. I am sorry, military training kicked in.'

'Your bloody elbow.'

'I thought you were about to attack me.'

'In a bloody public toilet in Morpeth?'

'Hold still. Let's stop the bleeding.'

The toilet door opens slightly, the dude dressed like a country squire who was messing with a newspaper crossword is about to step in, sees bloody Callum, and steps out again before Mike can explain it's an accident.

A few minutes later the bleeding stops, Callum, recovered from his initial shock, is cleaning himself up.

Mike is apologising profusely, and Callum is telling him not to worry about it. Maybe he shouldn't have touched a jumpy man on the shoulder, but he didn't expect to be assaulted after having a number two in the loo.

Callum holds his right hand for Mike to shake as they establish eye contact for the first time. Mike estimates he's a good fifteen to twenty years older than him. He refuses the hand of friendship for hygienic reasons.

'Wash them properly if you've just done a shite,' says Mike, thinking they can talk about Lisa's things now they've bumped into each other.

'Why are you paying off that hack, son?'

'Protecting your daughter's name.'

'No need, that's the good Lord's job.'

'A bit late for that.'

'Aren't you protecting your own name too? What's your story? What secrets reside inside that damaged head that smacks people in the kisser for absolutely no reason at all?'

'I said I am sorry. How many apologies do you want?'

Callum runs his hands under the dryer, shaking them like an American deep south evangelist on TV praising the Lord and begging for funds. There's still no mention of any instruments or the rest of Lisa's belongings.

'I like you, an optimistic pessimist. You're hurting big time. Not just the scars, but spiritually, son. Take the pledge and join the Brotherhood.'

'You're OK. I've got a father, Jimmy. Lives in Berwick with my mum,

Linda. Sorry to say, I am not your son.'

'We should go out for a meal in Morpeth when this is over, long as you promise not to attack me again for no reason. I am sure we will find we have a lot in common. Lisa's friends will all be there too.'

'Sally Palmer?'

'Dear girl lives in a fantasy world. Fingers in the bum. That's not a normal way to behave, is it?' asks Callum.

'I don't know. What do you and the wife do?'

'Strictly missionary, nothing abnormal.'

'Did Lisa ever tell you about any sex abuse she suffered at school and college?'

'Of course not, Lisa was sent by God to enhance our lives, not to lead men into temptation. Anyway, she's not dead. The Brotherhood believes when a person dies their existence ends until the day of resurrection when Jesus Christ returns to earth. I quote, *Mark 16:16: He that believeth and is baptised shall be saved; but he that believeth not shall be damned.*'

'Lisa's lack of faith killed her?'

'Don't be silly.'

Petty explains that the Lord works in mysterious ways. Everything happens for a reason, and he cannot second guess his Lord, nor should anyone else. He punishes the guilty in his unique way. Nobody escapes his wrath. He invites Mike to sit closer to them in the courtroom, he'll feel warmer spiritually.

'What time exactly is the Lord planning to return?'

'No need to be sarcastic. We'll pray that you find a new way.'

'I have a clear conscience, and prayers are like pissing into the wind, no offence,' lies Mike.

'None taken, son. The offer — and my heart — is always open. You'll always be in our prayers. Take the pledge anytime you want.'

Despite the invitation, Mike sits in his original seat when the inquest resumes. Nobody mentions Callum Petty's damaged beak.

Cavendish calls the next witness, a young police officer in uniform.

DC Sophie Trent swears to tell the truth and states she used to work for the Northumberland police's sex crimes unit. She investigated both of Sally Palmer's abuse claims having been assigned the cases by her sergeant, DS Connie Beach. They were seen as separate unrelated cases, two for one. Sophie says they — her colleague from the Berwick police station and herself — are both wearing dress uniforms out of respect for poor Lisa, the deceased.

I'm listening to her, thinking what is an unserious sex crime, same way as people are a little racist, or a little homophobic or transphobic. Like soldiers go into war and must differentiate between legitimate targets and innocent civilians. Difficult when they are dressed the same and can kill you in the blink of an eye. Kill and capture helicopter nighttime assaults against suspected Taliban were carried out at pace and collateral damage was impossible to avoid without risking your own life.

She says her testimony only deals with Lisa Wright's situation, not Sally Palmer's case. She says although Sally Palmer's evidence reporting rape, sex abuse and underaged sex was credible, they needed a statement on the record from Lisa Wright outlining to the police exactly what the two adults had done to her. Part of her job was to win Lisa's trust and get a video statement that could be used in court. They needed specific allegations to put to the accused that weren't based on the anecdotal evidence of a third party who wasn't there. According to Sophie, there was one major problem. Lisa wasn't keen on talking about any abuse or underage sex with her teachers.

Without denying or confirming any of Sally Palmer's allegations, Lisa was simply concerned about whether the CPS could go ahead with a prosecution without her. How could that happen, if all they had was the evidence from a jealous former friend. Lisa said Sally Palmer was making it up because she had a successful music career with the Great Northern Philharmonic Orchestra while her silly idiot friend was just an amateur musician who changed bedpans to pay her rent.

I look over at Sally while the detective constable testifies and the word stoic springs to mind as yet another witness — this one her dead best friend, Lisa Wright — undermines her credibility from beyond the metaphorical grave. She must be hating me after my testimony.

Sophie says at the initial police interview, she and Lisa spent three hours chatting without talking about abuse. Lisa was interrogating her with *what if* questions. Lisa was only really interested in protecting herself and making sure she was not going to be identified by her name or appearance in court or in the media. *What if* she didn't make a statement, could they still prosecute? Yes. *What if* she did make a statement, could they identify her in court? No, the police could protect her identity. *What if* the media reported her name and occupation? The law protects victims, and the media are not allowed to report anything that might identify her. *What if* social media broke the rules? The same applies, they would be in contempt of court and face possible criminal prosecution. What about other countries? British laws don't apply overseas. *What if* other victims came forward? That would be good, because the more solid the evidence, the better the chances of locking them up. But the police need Lisa's statement first before they can cast out the fishing net and go trawling for other victims. *What if* she walked away today and never came back. The detective told Lisa they would still investigate them and build a case, with or without her. *What if* they arrested them and they say she was asking for it, begging it, enjoying it?

Sophie said it was not unusual for survivors to feel that way when they have been groomed and emotionally manipulated. At the end of the interview, Lisa said she needed more time. Sophie told her to take her time because it was a big step. But in the meantime, avoid any counselling until after a trial because the defence would always say that Lisa's memories had been deliberately warped. She hated saying it, but Lisa needed to be warned. Any case would get ugly, but she wouldn't be alone.

Cavendish thanks her and asks does she believe Lisa's story?

'I believe all complainants until they give me a reason not to. And it's very rare to have false allegations. As far as I was concerned Lisa's reluctance to talk was not unusual. Not many people can spill the beans by clicking their fingers and letting the words flow like water from a tap. It is a traumatic experience reliving historic sex abuse and Lisa's reluctance was normal.'

'But no statement, no case?' asks Cavendish.

'We were playing a long game to ensure nobody else was hurt.'

'And what did that involve.'

'We interviewed the accused under caution without arresting them.'

'The Brays.'

'Yes, the Brays.'

'Why?'

'Scare them into stopping.'

'Did they confess?'

'No. They denied everything. Whoever made the claims was a fantasist. They were religious people who loved God.'

'Plausible?'

'No comment. We interviewed the head of the college and asked if he had any evidence of staff abusing pupils and students and he said they had none and everyone was vetted and checked before they were employed,' says Sophie.

'What did you hope would happen?'

'Over time Lisa would trust me enough to give me a video statement.'

'And how did that work out?'

'I spent six months chatting to Lisa, meeting up with her several times, until...'

'Until?'

'Her alleged abusers died,' says Sophie.

'What did Lisa say when you told her?'

'Nothing much, we only found out a couple of weeks after it happened. I think she asked if that was the end of our investigation. I said yes, and she thanked me, talked about fate forgiving nobody, and simply left the room.'

'Did she ever mention suicide to you?'

'No.'

'In any context?'

'No.'

'Thank you for your testimony, DC Trent. We have a few questions from the floor.'

First up the Petty duo repeat their forgiveness spiel, absolving the police of any blame into the death of their daughter.

Second up, Sally Palmer asks did the police believe Lisa had been abused despite her never making an official statement?

Trent repeats she believes all complainants until they give her a reason to disbelieve them.

Sally follows up with another: would the police and CPS have taken the Brays to court on her evidence alone?

Sophie shrugs and says nobody will ever know.

'But you believed me?'

'Yes.'

'Thank you.'

Finally, the small lawyer Burr asks questions requiring simple yes or no answers as the inquest deals with facts, not speculation.

'Did Ms Wright ever mention she had been sexually abused by anybody?'

'No.'

'Did the police ever mention the complainant and the accused by name when they spoke to the school and the college?'

'No.'

'Did the police ever contact the head administrator of the Great Northern Philharmonic Orchestra?'

'No.'

'Why not?'

'I can't answer that yes or no!'

Burr apologises and says he will rephrase the question.

'You agree there was no need to contact the Great Northern Philharmonic Orchestra because it wasn't connected to the abuse of Ms Wright?'

'Yes, I agree.'

'Nor did they employ the accused in any capacity?'

'Yes, as far as I am aware.'

'No further questions.'

Cavendish thanks the young police officer for her time and spends a few minutes looking through her papers before calling the second police officer to the stand.

The new witness identifies herself as WPC Zoe Chandler, stationed in Berwick. She says Lisa's postmortem revealed she suffered massive blood loss, multiple organ failure, and severe brain trauma from her fall. The toxicology report revealed small traces of alcohol, cocaine and Prozac, but not in sufficient quantities to have caused the fall. The weather conditions were normal for the time of year and were safe for experienced runners and hikers. WPC Chandler said she also spoke to the family and friends of Lisa Wright to ascertain if she had any reason to feel suicidal or whether she had a problem with drinking. Only Ms Palmer was concerned about her state of mind. Nobody else mentioned it. Lisa's online platforms showed no interest or searches for anything connected with suicide or self-harm. She was mainly interested in music and athletic events in Berwick and Northumberland, nothing to suggest she was planning to hurt or harm herself. Her flat was searched the day after her death for a suicide note and nothing found, there was no stockpile of drugs or anything else to suggest she had an exit-pack hidden away.

Cavendish thanks WPC for all her hard work and says they will hear from the last witness before they break for lunch. Afterwards, they will hear from the head administrator from the Great Northern Philharmonic Orchestra and a counsellor who worked with Lisa prior to her accident.

I know it is only a slip of the tongue from Cavendish, but I also know she has already made her mind up about the unexplained cause of death and WPC Chandler had just confirmed the reasons why. Cavendish was rushing through the evidence and knew that there would not be any way of proving Lisa deliberately took actions to end her life on top of the cliffs. Whatever anybody said, it would be impossible to prove what was happening in her mind. I'd spoken to Chandler, and it had been amicable. We were friends and ran together occasionally. She never mentioned Lisa's drunkenness and wild behaviour around town because she is a good egg and doesn't want to denigrate the dead when they cannot defend themselves. Lisa wasn't a cutter or a cry-for-help-merchant. Chandler wasn't looking for extra work or overtime. She was a good community copper. I'd thank her next time I saw her on patrol in Berwick.

Lisa's GP, Helen Bishop, says, according to historic notes, Lisa's anxiety issues started with her sacking from her job as a professional musician with the Great Northern Philharmonic Orchestra and she was prescribed Prozac to cope with the stress. Although she was only her doctor for the six months she'd been in Berwick, there hadn't been any previous ongoing anxiety issues on her record as a child, teenager and a young woman.

Cavendish asks what was Lisa like when she met her? Did she become more anxious over the six months she was registered with the surgery?

The GP shrugs, they'd never had a face-to-face as the diagnosis was carried online via an e-consult referral system managed by nursing staff.

Cavendish asks if it is usual for the GP's surgery to do things remotely without seeing the patient in person.

'We do our best, but we have thousands of patients and limited appointments. Lisa Wright didn't have a history of anxiety, self-harming or other red flags. There is no mention anywhere about mental health or sex abuse referrals. Certainly, she was never suicidal. We've all heard the evidence today. I've walked along those cliffs. They are dangerous if you don't like heights. And it gets very windy in Berwick. If you asked my own opinion, it was a foolish place for Lisa to go out running when she was pregnant.'

'What do you mean?' asks Cavendish.

'The post-mortem report says Lisa was three months pregnant at the time of her death. My apologies, as I've explained, the information wasn't on the first report. A clerical error. Poor proof reading.'

'Thank you, Dr. Bishop, you're free to go. I'd like to recall Mr Nicholls briefly after lunch.'

I am fuming as I watch Bishop and her colleague leaving the inquest and wonder why she became a doctor in the first place. There is no anger because one of their patients died an unnatural death. No acknowledgement they could have done more. No apology to the friends of Lisa Wright, just casual indifference. It's like joining the Marines and being surprised when they ask you to kill brown people with your bare hands. The doctor is probably happy as long she gets her three holidays a year. She has a dig at me, and she won't be the first or the last. Lots of people in Berwick are blaming me for the accident, although not too many will say it to my face. They aren't brave enough to accuse me directly. I didn't know Lisa was pregnant, but the coroner is going to ask if it was mine. That's why she wants me to stay a little longer. Is it mine? I cannot say yes or no. Only perhaps.

4

Outside with forty-five minutes to kill, Mike goes to his black Tiguan parked in the county council's car park. He's brought two smoked salmon and goat's cheese bagels and a flask of freshly ground coffee for his lunch. Cheaper and healthier to prepare his own food.

Mike opens the door and settles into the driver's seat. Unlike Berwick, there's not a windchill factor bringing down the temperature forcing him to shut the doors to stay warm.

He can go home now and avoid being interviewed about pregnant Lisa. Everything is settled, the inquest a forgone conclusion. Lisa's nightmare is not going to be exposed despite the efforts of Sally Palmer to seek a retrospective justice. A dead baby doesn't change anything.

All he needs to do is put the keys in the ignition, start the car, release the handbrake and put his foot on the accelerator and drive away from the woes of Lisa Wright.

A car three spaces down from him flashes orange hazard lights. Sally Palmer is pointing a fob at a three-year old red Audi TT Roadster soft-top, a zippy boy racer.

She notices him and smiles.

'Not having lunch with the girlfriends of Lisa Wright after your exhausting session, more tiring than having real sex?'

'Not been invited,' laughs Sally with a smile, lifting her left arm and smelling under her armpit, pulling a face. Sniffs her fingers. Pulls another face. 'Smokers are universally hated. Fingers stink of nicotine. So are insensitive jerks like you.'

He says he'll share his lunch with her before he heads off home. He's seen and heard enough. She climbs into the seat beside him and pulls her dress down to cover exposed thighs. He unwraps the bagels from the tin foil. She takes one and has a big bite. He does the same, checking her exposed flesh around her face, neck and shoulders for bruises.

Is she into the same alleged masochistic sex games as Lisa was?

'You've got to stay to answer the coroner's questions. Otherwise, you'll be in contempt of court. Besides, the counsellor Simon Lord will be testifying, and he will be exonerating me when he explains how he was helping Lisa tackle her sexual abuse at the hands of the Brays. Simon will prove to the world I am not responsible for the death of my best friend.'

'You are a bit responsible, you grassed her to the police' says Mike, instantly regretting his bluntness after her graphic testimony.

'Why? Better to pretend nothing ever happened, like you.'

'For Lisa's sake, yes.'

'It's never that simple, she could never push it to one side. Even with tainted eye candy like you to distract her.'

'What do you mean?'

'You're the sort of man Lisa likes.'

'Disfigured and traumatised by war?

'No, confident in themselves. Your body language says an inner peace that most of us spend a whole life trying to find. You don't hide the scars on your face or your hands.'

'Flattery will get you everywhere.'

'A bottle of wine and a meal tonight? I don't want to go home alone, not after today's session. That was awful. And my husband's away at yet another crucial marketing conference. Empty flats are lonely places.'

'I am suddenly Mr Popular. My scars aren't putting people off. That's my second invitation today. Old man Petty invited me to join his wife and Lisa's girlfriends for tea in Morpeth.'

'That condescending freak show. They aren't Lisa's real parents, you know. They adopted her when Lisa's teenage birth parents died in a tragic accident poisoned by carbon monoxide in a caravan.'

'She never told me.'

'The Pettys are as mad as a box of frogs. They run a religious retreat for The Brotherhood of Jesus on the England-Scotland border. Their cult preaches dead people go into an unconscious state from which only true believers will be resurrected clean, healthy and happy during the second coming of Jesus. Unbelievers, they say, will be punished for their previous crimes on earth and return with physical, mental and economic disadvantages. Isn't that nuts?'

'Lisa never mentioned either set of parents to me.'

'But she did tell you the other stuff, the Brays' sex abuse? Did you sign a pledge like everyone else? Lisa likes her written lists.'

'Eat your food. And stop fishing. I told my truth at the inquest.'

Sally snorts at him as if to say she doesn't believe him. She chews loudly, enjoying every mouthful.

'That bagel was great. Did you make it or is there a Mrs Mike Nicholls at home doing the hoovering and looking after the kids while you play away?'

'I'd not inflict my lifestyle choices on a wife and kids.'

'The scarring? Do you ever talk about it? Were you near to death?'

'Just an accident, a miscalculation and piss poor planning, a lot of it down to me. I accept full responsibility.'

'Why don't you wear a hat to hide your scars? Most men would.'

'Why? I am not ashamed of how I look. A wee Scottish barber in Berwick called Innes Grey shaves my head twice a week, I am as bald as he is. If it grew out on half my head, I am ginger like you.'

'Wish I met you before I married Ian, although you're probably a figment of my imagination and I am an early menopause victim. Not blaming others for your misfortune. Just like Lisa. Saying that, you are a cock getting Lisa pregnant.'

Mike ignores her dig, smiles and keeps it civilised, changes the subject and says that it's not normal for women to flirt with men nearly twenty years older than them, especially when they had goat's cheese in the corner of their mouth.

She licks it away while he reaches for the glove compartment for a small bag of tissues.

Too late, he remembers the book is in there too.

She sees and grabs it playfully, unaware of its relevance.

'What's the book? I love reading. I run a book club. *Angel Face* by J.D. Hammerhead? A best-selling Amazon erotic thriller? Never heard of it before. Crikey, Mike, I thought you had better taste, Cormac McCarthy, Elmore Leonard, Jimmy Thompson, or James Ellroy. Literary noir for real macho men.'

She is about to turn over the book to read the back cover blurb, but Mike snatches it and returns it to the glove compartment.

'It's not mine. My girlfriend Rhoda says it's a good holiday read. We should be heading back for the second half.'

'Can I borrow it?'

'Why?'

'I like erotic thrillers.'

'A finger up the bum?'

'Yes, that sort of shit.'

At least they have dark humour in common.

Mike's still laughing to himself back in the courtroom when everyone resumes their usual places.

He looks at Sally, finger jabbing at the mobile in her palm. She's a smart cookie; she's made the connection and she's probably ordering J.D. Hammerhead's *Angel Face* right now. He'd been a fool leaving the book in the car. She's not just buying a copy, she's reading the back cover blurb, and the online reviews on Amazon and GoodReads. Is she discovering J.D. Hammerhead has written a whole series of erotic thrillers following the same narrative arc; young girl comes of age sexually at the hands of a domineering older person or couple. The latter teach their professional virgin the art of making love where it is impossible to distinguish between pleasure and pain. They are absolute trash, but they sell, according to Amazon's best seller lists. Others that Hammerhead's penned include *Sugar Smacks* about a young actress and an older actor and actress, *Bone Spurs* about a doctor, matron and a nurse's daughter, *Candy Can*, the same story as Lisa's but starring pop musicians on tour, a showbiz family with a backing singer still at school, and *Honeypot*, about a farming family who keep bees.

Is Sally making the connections?

That could be a big problem because that's Lisa's copy, not Rhoda's.

Rhoda doesn't exist, except she was a singer in the Specials AKA and the Bodysnatchers and sang *The Boiler*, a song about rape that could only be listened to once.

If Sally does make the connections, then she's going to be certain he's been lying in the witness box. He closes his eyes briefly and thinks back to that horrendous day, worse than any battlefield.

Lisa is half an hour late for our training session and I think I'll run towards her flat in Mount Street and meet her half-way. We could go up North Road and cut across the golf course and pick up the coastal path to St Abbs, near Eyemouth.

I don't meet her half-way as I anticipate and run up to a Mount Street terrace. There are two entrances, the front door and the back where there is an outdoor metal staircase.

I open the back gate and sprint up and knock. There is no answer so I peer through the window, for one second fearing she may have fallen or had a heart attack. That's being daft, she's fit as a fiddle.

Then I see the noose on the living room door. Fortunately, her neck isn't in it.

I open the back door with two swift kicks. I enter the apartment, calling out her name and hear the toilet flush.

She comes out of the bathroom wearing unbuttoned green and white striped pyjamas. Her face red as a beetroot, eyes bloodshot and ming around her nose and mouth.

'What are you doing here?'

'What's going on?'

'None of your business,' says Lisa.

I grab the noose and grip it hard as if it is a whip.

'This makes it my business. What's going on?'

'Autoerotic asphyxiation. Heightens sexual arousal and makes my orgasms more intense. You want to join me? You'll come, watching me come with my head in the noose,' says Lisa, grabbing for the rope with one hand and striking me several times with the other. Her punches bounce off me.

'What have you taken? Do you need to be sick? Shall I call an ambulance?'

'Get out of my flat and my life.'

She's about to start banging her head against the wall. I grab her wrists and bear hug her, a reverse Heimlich manoeuvre to dislodge the demons trapped inside her head. She is trying desperately to break free. Charlie Cortez would, ironically, put her in a strangle hold and cut the oxygen off from her brain.

There is a better, safer option.

'OK, no ambulances. Let's calm down and have a cup of tea?'

Almost every crisis in the world can be solved with a five-minute tea break, including this ridiculous cack-handed seduction from a highly agitated friend.

'Let's do what they do in this book! My pain is our pleasure,' screams Lisa.

'What book?'

'Angel fucking Face.'

'Tea. Then book club. Stop wrestling with me.'

The energy to fight dissipates and she sobs in my arms.

Ten minutes later, we are sitting in her living room, drinking wine and smoking weed and listening to Neil Young's Cortez the Killer endlessly on repeat, they came dancing across the water. On the coffee table, J.D. Hammerhead's erotic thriller, Angel Face, holding the secrets to Lisa Wright's universe.

She explains the piece of shit book is literally her story about how a talented young teenage musician was abused by her music teacher and his wife. Yes, they have different names and physical appearances in the book, but in real life the rapist and sexual predator are modelled on Bryan Bray, a teacher and composer at her music college and his accomplice, his pathetic wife, Betty Bray.

If ever Lisa went to court, they would run rings around her like they did with Frances Andrade, a fellow musician who took a fatal overdose of fluoxetine and insulin after multiple cries for help were ignored. They called Frances a liar and a barrister accused her of indulging in the realms of fantasy and telling a complete pack of lies. The judge said the barrister was not to blame for the suicide, although Lisa was not sure how that worked in the real world.

That's never ever going to happen to her. She would die first rather than face that humiliation of being called a liar and a fantasist.

'If anyone ever thinks this is me, Lisa Wright will be damaged goods for the rest of my life. Who will want to marry me? Love me? Give me children? Even if they did, I'll spend my whole life waiting for my kids to discover the truth.'

'I am so sorry, Lisa. What can I do?'

'Nothing. And everything. You've done more than enough. Nobody can ever know what happened to me. You must swear blind on your mother's and father's lives that you will never tell anyone about my abuse or talk or think about it, even if I am dead. Will you sign a piece of paper, not that it's worth anything. Everyone betrays you, whatever is written down.'

'You're not going to die.'

'We all die. Look at you. Your incident. You never talk about it. My abuse is the same. You shove your accident so far up your arse, it'll never see the light of day again. Do that for me too, please.'

'Sounds painful.'

'Better than the alternative.'

'What's that?'

'A very quick goodbye, a long walk off a short plank into the deep dark sea.'

That's silly talk, I say. I'll pledge to look after you.

'In writing?'

'Naturally.'

His train of thought about keeping his word is interrupted by Cavendish asking the next witness to confirm her name and occupation.

'Kaitlin Becker, Great Northern Philharmonic Orchestra based in Newcastle, but performing in the UK, Europe and Asia.'

'How did you know the deceased, Lisa Wright?'

'She was employed as a violist with the orchestra I manage.'

'How long did she play with you?'

'Ten years, I believe. I only joined seven years ago.'

'How was she perceived as a member of the orchestra?'

'A valuable player and a respected colleague. She was popular with her fellow musicians, wilder than most of them, but it takes all sorts to tango. A lot of the established players get married, have kids, lead normal, ordinary lives. Others remain hedonists.'

'Three years ago, you released her from her permanent contract. Why was that?'

'She was going off the rails. She was accumulating a track record of repeated poor behaviour, culminating in being drunk and unable to play during a performance of Shostakovich's *Fifth Symphony* in Newcastle. As far as the conductor and myself were concerned, that was the straw that broke the camel's back.'

'What happened next?'

'Afterwards, Lisa was unable to explain what happened to the conductor and myself and we agreed to place her on garden leave until her situation was fully investigated.'

'How was this done?'

'By email.'

'Not face to face?'

'She refused to come in.'

'In those emails you suggest she seeks mental health counselling at her own expense, and you also sent her a link to the Samaritans. Was that the extent of your safeguarding and duty of care to an employee?'

'Objection,' interrupts Becker's lawyer, Bob Burr. 'My client is not on trial.'

'We're investigating an unnatural death, Mr Burr. I am not criticising your client, just establishing the facts. What happened after you sent Lisa your emails?'

'She wrote back to me and said she was unwilling to be ridiculed by her colleagues and immediately resigned from the orchestra.'

'Did she stop playing music completely?'

'I don't know. I never spoke to her again.'

'Did you know about any sexual abuse claims around Lisa? Did you know the police were investigating sex abuse claims at Lisa's college?'

'No, but the music world is awash with sex stories, most of which are utter rubbish. Lisa had a reputation as a promiscuous drunk, so it was unlikely she was a victim the way she behaved with others.'

'Do you have any evidence about her promiscuity and drunkenness?'

'Not really, everyone knew what she was like. Ask her trainer friend over there.'

'How did you feel when you heard she had died?'

'Very sad, obviously, but she had left the orchestra for three years by then and she wasn't our concern anymore.'

'Her behaviour declined very rapidly in a short space of time, coinciding with her being a reluctant complainant in a sex abuse investigation. Weren't you curious as to the cause?'

'Objection.'

'Sit down Mr Burr.'

'I did everything by the book. Suggested counselling. Gave a link to the Samaritans. She resigned. We didn't sack her. She never told us about any personal problems. It was her failure to communicate, not ours.'

'But you didn't volunteer to pay for the counselling?'

'We're a professional orchestra, not a charity.'

'Thank you for your testimony.'

Cavendish opens up the inquest to the floor and Burr repeats most of the coroner's questions to ensure the inquest fully understands Becker is not at fault in anyway, whatsoever.

The Pettys forgive as usual, and Sally Palmer asks Becker if she ever received a letter from a rape crisis centre about the Brays?

Becker says no.

Sally asks if she remembers a short conversation they had at the Sage a short while after Lisa left the Great Northern players.

'No, again,' says Becker.

'I explained to you that Lisa deserved a second chance and there were extenuating circumstances behind her behaviour.'

'Did you? I cannot remember. I have thousands of conversations every week.'

'I strongly hinted it was to do with historic sexual abuse. Do you remember that?'

'Sorry, you were just another face in the audience talking loudly at me. I do my best for everyone in the orchestra, past and present.'

Cavendish says they can go and thanks them both for their time. She calls Simon Lord to the witness box and explains she will question him rather than let him read out his statement.

I look at the counsellor with the padded elbows on his jacket, placing the

'My name is Simon Lord, I am a qualified counsellor, working from offices in Morpeth and Alnwick.'

'How did you know Lisa Wright?'

'She was a client. I do pro bono work for people who cannot afford professional fees, but need my services and Lisa was one of them that met my criteria.'

'What's the other criteria?'

'Just the money,' says Lord.

'Who suggested her?'

'She approached me, I think.'

'No other checks?'

'Sally Palmer vouched for her. I do most of my pro bono work for specialist sex support services in the region.'

'Why sex abuse?'

'They need me the most.'

'How many sessions did you have?'

'Six 45 minutes sessions were booked. She could have had 20 in total over a 12-month period.'

'Did you keep notes, tape your sessions?'

'I kept brief notes but never recorded anything. Our conversations were strictly confidential.'

'What did she want to discuss with you?'

'Anxiety. Depression. Low self-esteem. Her drinking.'

'The sex abuse that Sally claims she suffered?'

'Normally I wouldn't talk about a client's life if she was still alive without her consent and I am aware that I must still respect her privacy. But what I can say, she was on the verge of turning the corner thanks to our positive relationship, until her continued heavy drinking and two missed appointments blocked our progress.'

'Was there ever any discussion of suicide?'

'No. Although she has a hedonistic personality, I would never say she was suicidal, angry yes, self-harming no. She was more upset about being fired from her orchestra than dealing with the sex crimes allegations.'

'Did you discuss sex?'

'Yes.'

'Her abuse?'

'No.'

'Why?

'None took place. She told me she only ever has consensual sex.'

'Did she mention the police investigation?'

'Only in the sense her best friend had betrayed her.'

'So, in your professional opinion, she was never a suicidal risk.'

'No. Accidents happen sadly. Maybe Lisa was misguided to run across the cliffs. I've seen them. They are intimidating if you don't like heights.'

'One more question, when did you last speak to her?'

'At the end of our last session, we never met again after that.'

'Did you find out why she missed the two sessions?'

'No, the bottle was more help than me,' says Lord. 'We can't save everyone, much as we try.'

Cavendish opens the floor, and the Pettys run through their forgiveness spiel. Sally Palmer remains seated, glued to her phone.

With no further questions from the floor, Cavendish recalls Mike and says he does not need to affirm he's telling the truth as the first pledge still covers him. She thanks him for his patience waiting but has a couple more questions.

'Fire away,' he says, still digesting Lord's evasive responses to Cavendish questions. Sally said he would confirm the abuse took place and he did the opposite, convincingly undermining her credibility.

'Did you know Lisa was pregnant?'

'No.'

'She never told you?'

'No. Her business, not mine.'

'Did she have a boyfriend or boyfriends in Berwick?'

'I don't know. Nothing to do with me.'

'Were you in a sexual relationship with her?'

'I don't see the relevance?'

'I am just trying to ascertain reasons why she might be unhappy.'

'I think sex abuse trumps pregnancy.'

'Did you make her pregnant?'

'Again. No.'

'Thanks for your time. You're free to go.'

Mike has always been free. He's his own man, like Lisa was her own woman, a free spirit running wild.

Who is the father? Her landlord, John Armstrong, the banker, and property owner, a big noise in Borders finance and an online advisor guaranteeing his clients whacking great returns for letting him invest their cash in his property portfolios. Armstrong had been taking advantage of Lisa's drinking when she first crash-landed in Berwick. He kindly let Lisa stay virtually rent free in one of his houses, although her housemates resented her practising her music three or four hours every day. That's why she was always knocking on my door. I took John for a midnight walk to the middle of the Royal Border Bridge. The two of us had a nice little chat about fidelity and plying traumatised women with drink. John cleared his mobile of images and videos that were bad for his health and agreed to honour his marriage vows as we looked down on the River Tweed flowing one hundred and twenty feet beneath us. It's a long way down. He agreed to swap her rented room for an apartment for the same price. Had he disobeyed me and continued their affair? There were other candidates too, she didn't spend her early months in Berwick practising her viola in the day and howling at the moon at night. They were normal flings, young men her own age. We talked openly about them on our runs, not snide clandestine affairs conducted on WhatsApp behind closed doors or in black Range Rovers or empty rentals. And then there was me. I didn't want to think about it. Too painful.

Cavendish invites the interested persons to pay tributes to Lisa.

The Pettys talk about Lisa's love of music and how they are proud she came into their lives after her poor parents passed. Lisa was — and still is — their angel from heaven, loved and respected by people and many friends in music across the globe. The Pettys forgive everyone, noting that what looks like an easy route across cliffs for a tough ex-soldier may have been a step too far for a girl not used to such rugged terrain, not that they are blaming Mr Nicholls.

Claudia Popp, the nominated spokeswoman for the girlfriends of Lisa Wright, says they've lost a special friend, but God has gained a happy girl. She says she hopes the cliffs in heaven are a lot safer.

An hour later at 5pm on the dot, Cavendish announces her conclusion. An accident. Thanks everyone for attending. Explains the admin documentation process for interested persons. Closes the inquest and retires as everyone stands as a mark of respect.

Outside the courtroom the friends and family of Lisa Wright hug and shake hands and smile with relief that it isn't suicide.

Mike and Sally circumnavigate the group to walk to the car park. They are several paces apart and don't talk to each other, lost in their own thoughts. Recovering from their respective ordeals in the witness box, reliving bad memories that may or may not fade with time.

He's getting in the car, ready to drive home to Berwick on the racing circuit that is a single lane A1 where everyone drives safely apart from the reckless few in a rush to get to hell. If he had a quid for every time a politician promised to dual the road, he'd be a rich man.

She knocks on the car window, bending down so he can see who it is. He winds it down, his scars hidden from her view, a true pretty boy.

'Happy?'

'Not really,' says Mike. 'She's still dead. I thought running and exercise were good therapy. How could I be so wrong?'

'No, you weren't. We're both guilty of letting her down in our different ways, decisions made with the best of intentions.'

'And that lot?'

Mike nods his head towards the front of the council building housing the courtroom. The Pettys and the friends of Lisa Wright and her counsellor are still congratulating themselves. The coroner had said there has to be factual evidence to show Lisa intended to end her life and there was none. Soon they'll be in Morpeth toasting Lisa in a pub or a restaurant, a miserable setting to end a miserable day. Morpeth is probably the most miserable town in Northumberland.

Sally is looking in the same direction and snorts.

'They are delighted with an accident, nobody to blame.'

'Nothing is ever an accident — everything happens for a reason,' says Mike.

'Like her getting up the club? An accident?'

'Nothing to do with me,' says Mike.

'The book in your glove compartment? Is that a pure co-incidence, another so-called accident?' asks Sally. 'I downloaded a kindle version, started reading it in the inquest. Salacious shite, but it could be Lisa's story. How did the writer get hold of it? Did the graphic details float into his imagination like a bird of prey flying over a field?'

'You? Me? Police officers? Her parents? Who else knows her story?'

They both look at Simon Lord, the counsellor who has ditched his crossword puzzle and is joking with the friends of Lisa Wright. Sophie Trent, the young detective who investigated the original sex abuse allegations, is taking a photograph of the group, probably be on their socials within minutes as they spread the good news to their followers and online chums: *Lisa's death is an accident, not our fault.*

'God knows the truth, according to the Pettys, he'll punish the guilty.'

Sally smiles and snorts simultaneously.

'Simon Lord needs an accident of his own, wipe that smug look off his face.'

'We live in hope,' says Mike.

'You are a wry son of a bitch, despite lying to the court. I don't blame you for protecting her.'

'Great, I can put you down for a character reference next time I apply for a job.'

She pulls a face that says whatever.

'You know Simon Lord is lying through his back teeth.'

'Client confidentiality. That's a good thing. Like confession for

Catholics.'

'Maybe. Would you do me a great favour?'

'What?'

'Show me where she died on the cliffs so I can say goodbye properly.'

'When?

'Now. I'll just cry by myself all night if I go home alone. Ian will be at his conference trying to shag anything with a pulse. He has manhood issues.'

Mike has nothing better to do and would welcome the female company to unwind. Maybe they can help each other lessen the guilt they are feeling. She is exhausted after her intense testimony. He could ask about the two would-be rapists, aka Ben and Colin. Find out who they really are, uncover their real names. Pay them a visit with Charlie Cortez. She could tell him more about spineless Simon Lord as well, find out why a man thinks it's OK for a male to be counselling female sex victims and selling their sessions to anonymous authors.

'I'll buy the fish and chips from Coulls and we can eat them overlooking the ocean and say goodbye to our friend. Come on, follow me.'

OFF
THE
RECORD

5

She walks in beauty, like the night
Of cloudless climes and starry skies;
And all that's best of dark and bright
Meet in her aspect and her eyes;
Thus mellowed to that tender light
Which heaven to gaudy day denies.

They are alone, nine at night and the sky is cloudless, bright and as blue as the sea below. The tide is halfway in and halfway out, the estuary neither empty nor full. Their panoramic view shows the slight curve of the earth where the sky meets the sea. Miles across the water a minuscule vessel is heading to Scotland from Europe.

Standing straight and tall on the cliff top where Lisa fell, they silently breathe sea air deep into their lungs. They savour the space around them after the claustrophobic intensity of the Cavendish inquest.

Only the wind reminds them they are in Berwick.

Sandy beaches either side of them are empty apart from a few isolated dog walkers wandering close to the incoming waves, grabbing the last of the light before darkness descends. The paved promenade is empty. It's late May and the holiday season in Berwick is yet to get serious when the town's population doubles and the caravan parks and second home rentals are fully booked. Berwick is the happiest place to live in the country, according to a national newspaper. Mike's not sure what criteria they used. Berwick insiders, himself included, are not particularly demonstrative people. Happy is not their default setting.

The two of them are licking their lips silently, like cats and dogs after they've been fed. The fish and chips from Coulls in Castlegate had been delicious. They also bought and drunk two mini bottles of white wine sat on an ancient stone wall where they could toast a lost friend.

They'll be still under the limit when they get in his car to drive home. They've already agreed Sally is going to kip at Mike's for the night. She's taken two days off work for the inquest and it's a long drive in the dark to miserable Morpeth, even though she's no slouch behind the wheel of her Audi. She was up his backside most of the trip home, pushing him to go faster.

They finish their meal and pack the litter away. Sally recites a poem and Mike listens to her words about walking in beauty, like the night …and all that's best of dark and bright. Standing close to the edge of the cliffs, she shouts her words into the wind, directing them towards Scandinavia five hundred miles away to her left. Are they listening in Farsund, thinks Mike. Is his good friend and Viking warrior Tore Torson Galdal listening? In a crisis there was no better man to have by your side. But that's another story.

When she's done, Mike asks if she wrote the poem and she laughs and says, no, a mad, bad wordsmith called George Gordon was the guilty party. He's better known as Lord Byron. He wrote *She Walks in Beauty* after bumping into a stunning married woman at a society party in London and falling in lust.

'Every woman should have a love poem written about them, one that celebrates them in words and images,' says Sally, spreading her naked arms into the sky. 'Have you ever fallen in love when you shouldn't have?'

'Plenty of times,' says Mike, mirroring her movement in slow motion, the sleeves of his shirt rolled up, his tie flapping in the wind, remembering dancing to the Fine Young Cannibals' version of the Buzzcocks' punk classic. Disturbing natural emotions, feeling dirty and hurt, indeed. Thanks Lisa.

'Good or bad?'

'Both. You?'

'Not as much as I'd have liked. Do you think Lisa ever loved someone? Or was loved?'

'I don't know.'

His reply, as usual, is the equivalent of a forward defensive prod when a new batsman is playing himself in, getting used to the pace of the pitch. She drops her arms, and he follows. They do a few breathing exercises as the wind gently buffets them on the deserted clifftop.

'I can understand why you lied to protect Lisa's reputation but why are we giving Simon Lord and J.D. Hammerhead a free ride.'

'You're speculating,' says Mike. 'And since when did you and me become 'we'?'

'Only two of us care about her.'

'We're here to say goodbye to Lisa, not reopen old wounds,' says Mike.

'We take the blame for no reason.'

She has a point, although it's never black and white. She told the police and ruined Lisa's life, and he took Lisa on a death run. Except Lisa was doing alright until she read *Angel Face* and her carefree grin vanished overnight. She was coping with Sally's betrayal. Her abusers were dead. There was no police case to scare the life out of her. She was practising the viola again. She had a future.

'What do you want to do about it?' he asks.

'Find the truth.'

'And then what? You know the lads who assaulted you. Did you do anything? Revenge is great in theory, but not in practice.'

'Not enough evidence for a successful prosecution, too much reasonable doubt,' says Sally.

'Maybe it is for the best,' says Mike.

'We should have a plan.'

'For the dudes who assaulted you? Do you know their real names?'

'I would rather talk about Simon bloody Lord and J.D bloody Hammerhead.'

Mike looks away from the Nicole Kidman lookalike.

'We should sleep on it,' says Mike.

'Together?' asks Sally, tongue in cheek to show she's joking, tacitly agreeing to leave it for now as it's been a long stressful day. 'Can I have a moment alone?'

Mike steps back from the cliff's edge, retreats fifty yards to the stone wall and watches her go down on her knees and clasp her hands in prayer. Unlike the Pettys, she's not making a song and dance about her faith. He has no problem with people believing, just don't ram religion down the throats of everyone else.

He glances away from Sally and looks back over Berwick, once one of the most important strategic locations in the British Isles. The English and Scottish would regularly scrap over it and ownership of the town changed hands at least a dozen times several hundred years ago. Rumour has it Berwick was still at war with the Russians as the town wasn't included in the peace treaty that ended the Crimean war. Thankfully, the Ukrainian people were distracting Ivan big time. North Northumberlanders could sleep easy without drones dive bombing anyone beneath them like seagulls. Obviously, it was a good PR anecdote for tourists and travel journalists looking to pad out thin articles.

Why didn't J.D Hammerhead write historical novels rather than punting salacious violent porn cosplaying, stealing the victims' pain for commercial gain?

Sally was right. The least they could do was unmask the catalysts of Lisa's demise. They needed a plan and a strategy.

Like the one I had with wild Stevie Gannon, my fellow stunt man and former US Marine. A larger-than-life character, until he got unlucky in Kentucky. My careless friend slept off a massive hangover in the wrong place at the wrong time on the wrong midnight express line. Did Gannon hear the diesel drumming too late, running all down the line?

'Thank you.' Sally rejoins him after completing her quiet time vigil for Lisa. 'A penny for them?'

'We identify the author. And his or her source,' says Mike.

'Is that it?'

'What do you want? Blood? That's Charlie Cortez, not me.'

'Who is he?'

'My best friend. He believes in absolute vengeance, like that New Model Army song about killing the bastards.'

'Way before my time. Where does Charlie live?'

'In the wilderness, he has problems integrating.'

'Are you best friends, like me and Lisa?'

'I've never grassed him to the cops.'

'Ouch.'

'No offence. We'll start hunting at the White Owl tomorrow morning. Did you ever see Lisa in person after you snitched on her?'

Sally says no and looks out over the North Sea.

'How do you deal with them, Ben and Colin? How do get them out of your mind?'

'With difficulty.'

'Give me their names?'

'Why? What are you going to do if I tell you?'

'Nothing. Just a test. See if we can trust each other.'

'Tony Webb and Roger Worcester. Both doctors now. Fine fellows.'

Webb and Worcester, he'll tell Charlie. Sounds like a double comedy act on TV in the early nineties.

6

It's five in the morning and the bright light is beaming on Mike's face as he struggles to sleep in his terraced cottage overlooking the estuary on one side and Magdalane playing fields on the other. He's not thought about Stevie Gannon for a while and hates being held hostage. Rather than let bad memories fester and turn gangrenous, he gets up an hour earlier than usual and hits the road hard to run the stunt man out of his mind.

When he returns, Sally is already up and making freshly ground coffee with a French press. She's wearing one of his white tee-shirts as a short dress showcasing long legs.

She is making herself very much at home in his home. He excuses himself while he showers to wash away the sweat after his tough training run. He's pushed himself hard over the cliffs, punished his body to erase the shit messing up his head.

'Breakfast?'

'Cold porridge and fruit normally. I made a bowl for you last night after you went to bed. Thanks for the coffee.'

They eat outside despite the cold; she borrows one of his jackets to stay warm. They watch the Tweed and the numerous different species of birds that fly around the river.

'Will I see dolphins?'

'Only if they are chasing breakfast on the tide,' says Mike. 'Salmon, eels, shrimp, squid — they devour them whole without chewing. Greedy buggers, almost as bad as seals.'

'Did you and Lisa do this?'

'Did she stay over and share breakfast? No. She rented a place near the station,' says Mike.

He's not sure why he continues to lie about how close he and Lisa were. Was he protecting her or himself?

'What happened to all her stuff? Did the Pettys collect it?'

'I don't know. When she died, I talked to the police and coroner's office. No one ever contacted me from the family.'

When they finish eating, she asks if she can borrow his toothbrush. If it is electric, does he have an unused head?

She playfully asks if he has any clean ladies' underwear or female perfumes left behind from family and guests and one-night stands. She hadn't packed for an overnight stay when she left her house in Morpeth yesterday morning and she hates minging like a dirty stop out.

He laughs and says check out the third bedroom and see if any of Angelina's kit fits. There are spare tooth heads in the bathroom.

'Who is Angelina?'

'My sister. She stays when she visits from that London. She's got a job in the city and is doing alright,' he says, and spins another lie, this whiter than the rest because he's protecting his sister's right to privacy even though she has no capacity.

'How often does she visit?'

'Every now and then. She's a very busy successful woman. We're all proud of what she's achieved.'

'Is that you and her?'

Mike looks at the framed picture of the two of them in the back garden, the Royal Bridge in the background, Spot, the brindle staffie rescue, sitting at their feet.

'Yes. When I was a real pretty boy before the crash and the Marines.'

'You both look very young.'

'Sixteen me, fourteen her.'

Sally disappears into his sister's spare room and comes out smelling like Angelina, smiling like Lisa used to when she'd finished a run or a practise session on the viola: *was I the best? Only you were playing. But was I the best?*

'I borrowed her perfume, knickers and a cardigan. Is it OK?'

'Sure.'

'Have you thought more about your plan?'

'Keep it simple with minimum moving parts.'

Two hours later, they walk down Pier Road and under an old bridge into Berwick's modest town centre turning left into Hyde Hill and right onto Bridge Street, the town's tiny artisan retail district. Halfway down they turn left into a green-fronted building with ornate writing proclaiming all are welcome at the White Owl, England's northernmost second-hand bookstore. .

'Where do we start?' asks Sally.

'With Corrine,' replies Mike and he nods across the book emporium. 'She's a bookseller and a runner too. Her name is Mudd.'

'Why?' asks Sally, frowning.

'Look at the books,' says Mike, nodding towards a display near the door showcasing half a dozen titles from best-selling crime fiction author Corrine Mudd. The black and white noir seductress portrait looks nothing like the happy pretty-in-pink real-thing approaching them with a big cheesecake grin.

'Dick,' snorts Sally, under her breath.

Mike and Corrine greet each other with a hug, and he introduces Sally as a good friend of Lisa's and Corrine makes all the right noises about grief and time being a great healer.

'Sally wants to spice up her marriage and has been recommended *Angel Face* by a J.D. Hammerhead. We're also after *Sugar Smacks*? Or *Candy Can*? And the other two were *Bone Spurs* and *Honeypot*? Any ideas?'

Corrine asks them to follow her, and she'll see what she can find.

'What's he filed under?' asks Sally.

'Erotic fetish fiction, I would imagine. You might enjoy Gillian Anderson's *Want* more. Or Anais Nin's *Delta of Venus* or *Little Bird*, both published by Penguin. They are equally filthy, but Gillian and Anais are literary, not exploitative. Or try Maxim Jakubowski's *Just a Girl with a Gun* if you're into erotic noir, something rather particular.'

'Is that a genre?'

'It is now I've copyrighted it.'

'Do you know J.D., personally, is it he or she?' asks Mike. 'I looked him or her up online and it said he or she could be a north-east literary writer making good money out of popular erotic thrillers to blue rinse cruiser bunnies, whoever they are.'

'He or she probably writes under an alias because it's not cool to write about a young female being groomed by an older man for kinky underaged sex...some readers find it tough to differentiate the writer from the book. Like Morrissey and the Smiths.'

'You read any?' asks Mike.

'Not to the end. A few pages to get the gist. Badly written junk, not literature. Women writing about sex is different to men. J.D. is definitely male in my opinion.'

'How would I find out the real name of J.D.?' asks Mike.

'Why do you want to know?'

'Sally's a bit of book festival groupie. Likes to get her books signed by the authors. Makes them more precious and special.'

'I don't have a clue. He is keeping his identity a secret because it's good PR. A great guessing game. Like Banksy.'

'Someone must know?'

'His publisher? Definitely, his literary agent.'

'Can you find out who that is?'

'You're very demanding today, Mike.'

'Keeping it real, Corrine.'

'One job at a time,' says Corrine, busily scanning book spines and using steps to reach the higher shelves. Eventually, she finds four titles and hands them to Mike who passes them to Sally.

'How long would it take to write and publish a book like this? asks Mike, holding up his second-hand copies of *Sugar Smacks* and *Candy Can.*'

'Hammerhead has a traditional publisher so anything up to two years from delivery of the final manuscript. Indies move quicker.'

'We'll take them all. Could you find out his agent for us?'

Five minutes later, Corrine says Hammerhead's literary agent is Lucy Graham, a lovely horse-riding lass who works in London, but appears regularly as a guest speaker on the northern book festival and creative writing circuits. She has family up north. She's in Manchester with her demon dog client — James Ellroy — for a couple of days. Her husband was seeing him in Newcastle. Search for her online and find other dates. That's the only way to get to speak to them. It's a closed shop the rest of the time. The world is full of misguided fools who think they can win the lottery and write best-selling novels in their coffee breaks at work.

Outside with an armful of books, Sally snorts at Mike and rebukes him for taking the piss out of her. 'Spicing up my marriage. You have a nerve, Mike Nicholls.'

'I might have hit a raw one. Isn't your old fella wondering why you're not back in Morpeth?'

'I doubt it. We're going through a sticky patch, not really a patch, ever since Lisa really, he doesn't understand. He's lost interest in me. Says I don't turn him on.'

'More fool him. Let's stay focussed. If we get heavy, we'll scare people off. Keep it light-hearted and fun. We act like book geeks.'

'At my expense?'

'Seriously, stop being so easily offended. You're going to have a nightmare reading this shit, but you're an honorary Marine doing your duty.'

'Nice one. Will you do it with me?'

'Don't you have to go back to work tomorrow? The health service will be in crisis.'

'Too many jokes. I am being serious. I took the week off. How does the rest of your plan work?'

'Spot similarities with rape cases at the crisis centre, see if they were counselled by Simon Lord, find living witnesses and evidence the police and CPS cannot reject.'

'Thank you. You're really helping me with my guilt, implying my half-baked statement to the police about Lisa was pointless.'

'The blame belongs beyond us,' says Mike. 'How do you fancy a four-hour road trip to Manchester for a little chat with Lucy Graham. Let's find out J.D. Hammerhead's real name.'

7

Good evening peepers, prowlers, pederasts, panty-sniffers, punks and pimps. I'm James Ellroy, the demon dog, the foul owl with the death growl, the white knight of the far right, and the slick trick with the donkey dick. I'm the author of books for the whole fuckin' family, if the name of your family is Manson.

The rapt middle-aged balding male audience in Waterstones, Manchester, lap up the Demon Dog's fascism-as-performance-art opening sales pitch of the self-confessed alt-right literary heavyweight champion of the world. According to the publicity blurb, the American noir giant is six foot three, with strong eyes and a tall, gruff face. Mike reckons he's shrinking fast, and lost a few inches and pounds. Age catches up with everyone sooner or later, himself included.

Mike is sitting next to Sally. They are both exhausted having devoured four J.D. Hammerhead 75,000-word novels in two days since the White Owl visit, finally finishing them just before they drove the two hundred miles from Berwick to Manchester. Sally spots her, a tall willowy well-dressed lady at least a dozen years older than her profile photograph on the lit agency's website. She nudges Mike and whispers to him to check out the chick to his left. Mike does and gives Sally the thumbs up. They both sit through a reading and an interview by a Scouse academic who wrote a scholarly essay on his American hero.

When they open the questions to the floor, a young buck called Phil asks Ellroy if breaking into houses and sniffing women's underwear is part of the creative writing process. Ellroy says while smelling knickers is good backstory colour, never discount the value of a good literary agent and PR. He picks the best.

Mike and Sally kettle Lucy Graham, approaching the literary agent in a north-south pincer movement, encasing her between two bookshelves. They have agreed tactics before they approach. Mike says he will do shock and awe, and Sally intervenes as the voice of reason.

They introduce themselves using their real names and say they've had a great evening listening to James. They loved every second, but they really want to talk about J.D. Hammerhead because they want to turn his books into movies, not porn but classy erotica for the women who buy Gillian Anderson's *Want*.

Lucy's eyes glaze over, and Mike understands. Everyone she meets must pitch a book or film project. They'd rather get a publishing deal than fuck her. The literary agent says contact her office explaining who they are, their track records with films, the names involved, and the deal they are offering. Most importantly, prove they have the finance.

Mike pulls out his mobile, opens it and shows her his contacts list, featuring many familiar movies stars and directors from Hollywood.

'Are you questioning my credentials in the movies? Name me a director or a producer or an A-lister. I probably have their numbers in my phone. We'll call them now, if you want. But rather than interrupt busy shoots, I just want to know his real name, prove J.D. Hammerhead isn't a Gary Glitter or a Jimmy Savile fiddling kids. Sally thinks he a plagiarist and a paedophile.'

An insulted Lucy says J.D. is a very serious writer published by a reputable publisher and is represented by a prestigious literary agency. Their insinuation is defamatory.

'Why is he hiding under a pseudonym then?' asks Mike. 'Why are you ashamed of him, or her?'

Lucy tries to bypass Sally, who bursts into tears on cue.

'This book. *Angel Face*. It's not fiction. It's real. A literal transcript of my best friend's account of her abuse at the hands of two predators. She jumped off a cliff. Killed herself. I've still not changed my dress from the inquest three days. I bet I stink. Can you smell me?'

Lucy sniffs the air instinctively, blushes, and stops trying to break out of her cordon. She quickly delves into her handbag and brings out a tissue.

'I am very sorry, but you're talking to the wrong woman.'

'I am not. Do you want to see a picture of Lisa? She was pregnant you know. The father's...'

'I am sorry, but this is nothing to do with me,' says Lucy.

Mike backs off a couple of paces to look less intimidating. Sally's playing a blinder and has the literary agent's attention. Sally asks if Lucy has children. Lucy replies three daughters.

'How old?'

'None of your business.'

'Lisa was fourteen when she was first assaulted at a prestigious music school by her teacher and his wife. Are your daughters that age?'

'Not yet, but close. What has this got to do with me?'

Sally says if Lucy wants to know more about her abuse forget the court transcripts, just read *Angel Face*.

'It's a piss take, it is a satire on erotica, not to be taken seriously. The author is one of the greatest living satirists in the UK,' says Lucy.

'No, it's not. It's a transcript of my friend's abuse. Read them again and imagine this is happening to her, aged fourteen,' says Sally, holding up her mobile to Lucy, showing the two of them in school uniforms holding their instruments.

'What do you want from me?' asks Lucy.

'His name and your silence,' says Sally.

'If I give you his name, I'll be breaking client confidentiality...this harassment is...'

'We're going now. We apologise for approaching you like this.'

'It's OK.'

Mike intervenes, his early anger dissipated, he's busking. Says he was with Lisa when she jumped off the cliff. He never saw her leap because she was behind him. The inquest said it was an accident because they could not prove she deliberately tried to harm herself, but he knows she read this book a week before and it broke her. He tried to pick up the pieces and failed miserably. Should have got her help, but he thought more exercise was best for her. He was wrong. That's on his conscience for the rest of his life.

'I can't give you his name. I'd be sacked, writers must trust you.'

'That's why we've asked for your silence. We don't want J.D. We want to expose whoever leaked the sex abuse transcripts to him. That's all,' says Mike. 'Stop him doing the same to other girls.'

'Like you daughters and their friends. Are they musicians?' asks Sally.

'All my girls play. Tabitha is a flautist. Gemma violin. And Alison, the black sheep of the family, plays guitar and sitar.'

'No viola players? I used to play. Lisa was in the Great Northern Philharmonic Orchestra,' says Sally.

'I still can't give you his name,' says Lucy. 'No matter how much you guilt trip me.'

'Point him out to us,' says Mike.

'He's not here.'

'His book. Recommend one of his books,' says Mike. 'Pick one out for us to buy?'

'Follow me.'

Lucy goes down the stairs and quickly locates the English literature section. Picks out a book and hands it to Sally who studies the front and back covers and passes it to Mike. The book is called *First They Take Your Dignity*, the blurb says it is an award-winning classic satire about fagging at public schools by a much-respected literary establishment icon, Robin C Hamilton. The inside jacket says the jocular author lives just outside Duns in the Scottish Borders with his wife Irish poet Shannon K Moran, three children, and their dog, Patch.

'What's he like?'

'A great writer.'

'Why *Angel Face*?'

'Sells and makes him far more money than satire.'

'You said *Angel Face* was satire.'

'I've got to go now. Work to do. My lips are sealed,' says Lucy.

Mike and Sally step out into Deansgate, gridlocked with traffic on the roads and partying punters crowding the pavements.

The city's far more ethnically diverse than dear old Berwick. His hometown looks positively antiquated in comparison to modern, original Manchester. But Berwick doesn't have the same homeless problem with humans sleeping rough in retail shop doorways. Mike would give them all a tenner on the walk to the car parked at the top end of Deansgate, but he only has a hundred and twenty quid in cash.

'That went well,' says Sally. 'Can we trust her to keep quiet?'

'She's only interested in her kids and family. Publishing is a hobby for her. Her old man will be loaded or there is a family trust or an inheritance somewhere down the line.'

'You are so cynical.'

'Realistic. Life's a bitch if you're not born with a silver spoon. Tougher when you can only sustain yourself by the sale of your labour and you're only one missed pay cheque away from the street.'

'What happens next?

'You're going to try and identify living victims exploited by Hamilton's books.'

'Aren't we going to confront him together?'

'I am going to observe him for a bit.'

'Spy on him?'

'Watch him in his habitat.'

'Like David Attenborough?'

'Shall we eat before we go home? Shall we try Chinatown? Japanese. Thai. I know two great restaurants, one of each.'

'You been here before? I am a rarity, a Manc virgin.'

'A few memorable runs ashore with Drew, Ronnie and Big Al and the rest of the merry men.'

'Runs ashore?'

'Pub crawls.'

'Is this a date?'

'No,' says Mike.

'If it feels like a date...did Lisa ever say the same to you?' asks Sally.

'That's why it is not.'

'Were you in love with her?'

'Were you?'

8

It's 6am Tuesday and Mike has been hidden in the back garden of a literary establishment icon for 24 hours. Two and a half weeks since the inquest and a fortnight after he last saw Sally Palmer in the flesh, Mike has been watching the gigantic rotund figure of Hamilton from a distance in his car and now up close under a hedge.

He has a good picture of the writer's routine. Hamilton works in the morning, plays in the afternoon and has fun feasting in the evenings, hosting guests a couple of times a week on the patio. He plays nine holes of golf on a Monday and Friday, swims Tuesdays and Thursdays, tennis on a Wednesday. Weekends are for the family, gardening and trips out.

Robin C is probably in his early sixties but looks older. He's not kept himself in great shape. Shannon, his younger prettier wife, is mid-thirties, and is the opposite. They have three young children that she manages, ferrying them to and from junior school in a white Range Rover and supervising their social activities with other families in Duns and the surrounding area. According to the internet, her name is Shannon K Moran, a former Irish actress with serious literary credentials and has published a couple of acclaimed poetry collections. Again, according to the web, Hamilton has another grown-up family down south in the home counties, but they are estranged. He moved north to get away from them. His entitled first wife Sarah Jane has serious hereditary connections to the Windsors and even more serious trust funds invested in overseas tax havens.

The satirist is drinking coffee on the patio, several hundred yards away. He's wearing a gaping grey dressing gown, occasionally blowing open to reveal his tackle, balls hanging like overripe melons.

On the surface, Hamilton lives a normal privileged life where money gives him freedoms not afforded to common people like Mike's folks and family. There is no sign of his alter-ego J.D. Hammerhead leering at schoolgirls in Duns or bashing his bishop in his writer's cabin in the garden overlooking the Pentland hills.

Mike's been inside the spacious office, and it is kitted out better than his own house. A neat writer's gaff for a satirist, but not a sign of J.D. Hammerhead. Was Lucy Graham spinning him a yarn to get rid of him and Sally?

In the movies, a character like Mike would emulate his namesake Michael Caine in *Get Carter* and brutalise Hamilton to loosen his tongue, but torture could never really be trusted because people will say anything to stop the pain. Mike's seen torture in action in Afghanistan and Iraq and it made no difference. They never trusted the intelligence and did what they were going to do anyway.

Does he need any more intelligence before he makes contact? Sally's been on his case, calling him for daily updates and is keen for him to speed up the slow burn. He would have loved to see Simon Lord rock up in Duns, see the two of them exchange files, tapes and cash. That would simplify everything if their entire Lisa Wright conspiracy was handed to him on a plate.

Fat chance. That only happens in plot-driven crime fiction where intelligent post-modern ironic serial killers are being chased by dysfunctional cops with hearts of gold who love their mums.

Eight hours later, after a refresh and rinse at home in Berwick, he's back in Duns, parked in the swimming pool next to the town's rugby and football clubs, a few hundred yards from Hamilton's home.

Mike arrives five minutes before Hamilton and swims flat out for a hundred lengths in an outside lane, pleased to be exercising his body after his 24-hour undergrowth vigil. Hamilton is more sedate, swimming breaststroke at a leisurely pace, nodding to his fellow regular swimmers.

After their respective work outs, they shower and change in the dressing room. Mike makes sure Hamilton does not notice him or his scars as they get dressed.

Hamilton waddles over to his Tesla and struggles to fit in the car. Mike watches and slides effortlessly behind him when he reverses out of his parking space. Mike follows him to the exit to the A6105. Hamilton is indicating left to go into Duns rather than home. He does errands occasionally after his afternoon exercises before school runs gridlock the town.

Hamilton hesitates at the junction and Mike drives straight into the back of him, breaking a light and cracking the Tesla's bumper. He's out of his Tiguan in seconds, knocking gently on the window saying it is all his fault. They reverse their cars away from the exit to exchange contact and insurance details.

'I should really call the police. Report the accident,' says Hamilton.

'Please don't. Can I pay cash rather than lose my no claims?' asks Mike. 'Look, I am sorry. I wasn't paying attention. All my fault. My name's Mike. You are ...?'

'Robin.'

'I don't know what came over me. I thought...'

'Gosh, what happened to your head?'

Most people say nothing, look away immediately, embarrassed. The literary writer inside Hamilton cannot resist commenting.

'An accident on a movie set. I was a stuntman, and we got our timing wrong. Seconds, but it was enough.'

'How horrific. Must have been awful.'

'My Niki Lauda moment. What burns well with Shell? Mike Nicholls.'

'How can you joke about it?'

'You either laugh or cry.'

'What movie?'

'I signed an NDA in return for compensation. There's nothing on the internet. Just another one of Hollywood's secrets,' says Mike.

'Jesus. What a horrific story.'

'I don't talk about it. Too painful. Literally.'

'You should not bottle it up,' says Hamilton.

'Here's my card.'

Mike hands over his personal trainer business card with his contact details on and says he'll call him on his mobile, so he has his number. He'll get McCreath and Sons in North Road, Berwick to fix his own car. The Tesla is up to Robin, but he'll pick up the tab.

'Can I trust you?'

'I only live in Berwick. Born and bred. Everyone knows me. I am not going to do a runner for a couple of grand. I am a former Marine and stunt man. Not a petty criminal.'

'I live just up the road. We'll exchange details over a cup of tea.'

Ten minutes later Mike is formally introduced to Shannon sitting on the patio in baggy dungarees and crocs, reading. She welcomes the two men without any reaction to Mike's scars. Hamilton hugs his wife and furtively cups her left breast and vulva. The couple's age difference is huge, more like father and daughter than man and wife. Not that Mike's passing judgement. They are just numbers, everyone to their own.

They explain about the crash and how Mike is going to pay cash to repair the damage done to avoid losing his no claims bonus.

'You could pay some it off in kind,' suggests Hamilton. 'You're a trainer and Shannon and my doctors are always telling me to exercise more. I am pre-diabetes and am on bloody blood pressure pills, blood thinners and cholesterol. I rattle when I roll.'

'He won't change his diet,' says Shannon in a soft southern Irish accent. 'Stubborn as a mule.'

'Life's too short, Michael, I prefer full names rather than lazy abbreviations. You don't mind?'

'Sounds like a plan. We can run and do a few stretches for a couple of days, work out an exercise regime.'

'How much do you charge professionally?'

'Seventy-five an hour is the going rate for a top PT. I charged much more in California.'

'Jesus, you must be very good. A big come down from California to the Scottish Borders.'

'I am worth every dime,' grins Mike. 'In Hollywood I trained A-listers before becoming a stunt man. First names with lots of celluloid heroes.'

'What about me? I could lose a few pounds and tighten up the flabby bits. We need to look good for Glastonbury and Barbados,' says Shannon.

'You're fit enough already my sweet little pea with your childlike innocence. All my friends want to ride her. They can look but they better not touch, you included,' says Hamilton, the slightest hint of an inner Hammerhead breaching his upper middle-class cool.

'You're embarrassing the man, Robin. We have raucous parties, and his friends get very drunk and randy and, sadly, Robin encourages them to lust after his trophy wife. They don't see the irony that he's simply carrying out research into bad male behaviour.'

'Do you have the same problem with your female friends wanting to mount Robin and climb Everest?' asks Mike. For a second or two, he thinks he's totally blown it and squandered several grand. They are going to take offence, tell him to sling his hook and report the crash to the police.

'You'll be surprised at my pulling power,' grins Hamilton, 'I am well-schooled, St. Cuthberts, Marlborough and Cambridge. Intelligent women see beyond the physical attributes. You would have been a very pretty boy once, before your hideous injury. They can do wonders with plastic surgery nowadays. I am surprised...'

'Robin, leave him alone,' interrupts Shannon. 'Sorry, he's a terrible tease, even sober. One day he'll get punched in the nose, way he speaks without thinking. He thinks it's funny, when it's crass if you're not in on the joke.'

'Must knock your confidence when you're pulling chicks,' says Hamilton, like a dog with a bone refusing to let go.

'I might tell you about it one day. But not today. It's too painful and it would upset your wife,' says Mike, glad Charlie Cortez isn't taking part in the conversation.

Mike smiles at Shannon with her light green eyes, red hair and perfect skin, as if to say what can he do. He is making a secret connection with her. Does she know about Hammerhead? Would she bring up her own children knowing their father steals the stories of young sex abuse victims? Would she open-up to him if he gets close enough to her? Is she looking to escape an abusive, coercive, bullying relationship? Or is she complicit and laughing at him too.

There's only one way to find out, jump on board the Hammerhead express, see where the journey takes him.

'You can never be too fit, Robin. I am sure we can give Shannon a session or two,' laughs Mike.

'Thank you. I've heard British military training is the best,' says Shannon.

'Not in your part of Ireland you haven't,' says Mike.

'We're not all the same over there, are we, us Irish?'

'We have the same problems on the Berwick-Tweedmouth-Spittal border. More to do with pig-headedness than religion.'

She laughs. Hamilton laughs. Mike joins in too. Patch wags his tail furiously. Rabbits play mischievously from a safe distance at the bottom of the garden.

'I like you Michael, a stout fella. So does Patch.'

Mike asks what the two of them do.

'We're writers,' says Shannon.

'I am a satirist, fairly well known,' says Hamilton. 'The Times said my novel, *First They Take Your Dignity*, is still the most memorable unmasking of fagging in English public schools and hypocrisy, cronyism and sexual exploitation that are endemic within our most famous — and notorious — educational establishments.'

'Satire pays well, judging by the house and the land,' says Mike, giving an opportunity to introduce his alias, J.D. Hammerhead. 'How many books have you published?'

'Six,' says Hamilton. '*First* was my third. I am working on a follow-up. Halfway there. We are renting the house so I can focus on my writing. Too many distractions in London. My friends are riotous.'

'And you,' Mike asks Shannon, calculating there were at least half a dozen Hammerhead books.

'I am a poet. Pays less well, but the critics love me, and I take a good photograph if I suck my cheeks in, push out the chaps and add a bit of slap. The rest they can airbrush.'

They all laugh at Shannon's dry self-deprecating wit. Stand up and high five each other to show the new friends are bonding and are on the same wavelength. Did they do the same when they were plotting and planning *Angel Face*, laughing at Lisa Wright's torture and humiliation?

9

ike adds a couple of pieces of driftwood to the small fire on
Cocklawburn beach, the sea reflecting the glow of a blood red
sky as the sun goes down. Holy Island and Bamburgh are to his south,
Berwick and Scotland to the north and Sally Palmer is close by his side.
They are cooking salmon fillets and jacket potatoes wrapped in tin foil
on an iron griddle and sparingly sharing a bottle a beer. Both are driving
and have left their cars three quarters of a mile away.

'Missed you and your dry wit. Been over two weeks since we were last
together,' says Sally, unpinning her curly red hair and letting it cascade
over her shoulders.

'We've spoken on the phone,' replies Mike, staring at the flames and
enjoying the heat. His accident never made him nervous of fire.

'Not the same.'

'You're in a long-term relationship? What's his name?'

'Ian hasn't touched me much for months. Pressure of his marketing
job. Thankfully there are no kids or animals to fight over. One day I'll get
the energy to throw him out.'

'Not because of me,' says Mike. He doesn't want to have broken
relationships on his conscience alongside everything else. 'I am not on
the market.'

'Of course not, you're far too old and boring.'

'And I am heavily scarred. Looks shite in wedding photographs.'

'I don't see them anymore. Just you,' says Sally, gently stroking his arm that's prodding the fire with a stick and shifting the burning wood. 'You'd make a great dad, if you aren't one already.'

'I'll get some more fuel for the BBQ.'

He collects driftwood and glances at Sally, dressed in a wraparound dress and barefooted, her back to him facing the fire. He's unsure why she's still hanging around. What does she want from him? A relationship? Or justice for her best friend. Same as he does. She's naturally flirty, like Lisa. Doesn't know she's doing it half the time.

He throws more fuel on the fire and says the food's cooked. They add mayonnaise and pepper to the salmon steaks, cheese to the jacket potatoes and sit on a rug in the sand, using a large tree stump as a back rest.

'Did you do this with Lisa?'

'I've done this with lots of women over the years.'

'What a tart.'

'And men. How's your salmon?'

'You always have a smart answer to everything, yet you're also a closed book that you won't let anyone open. Not even the first page. Why?'

'There is nothing to say. If I unload on you, you'll share my misery for a while. Except you won't really, because you're not me, and you don't understand my life. Same with Lisa. I thought exercise would wash away her anxiety, make her feel good about her body and herself. I was wrong. You thought going to the police would stop the Brays from harming other kids and give Lisa closure. You were wrong too. The Brays' accident didn't change anything for Lisa. Her anxiety didn't disappear with the news, did it?'

'I don't know. We weren't speaking. The Brays got what they deserved. But this is a heavy-duty conversation for a beach BBQ with a mate.'

'You asked.'

'The food is going to get cold.'

While they eat, Mike updates her on the Hamilton surveillance operation. One or both of them will spill the Hammerhead beans.

'See, I told you, nothing is ever an accident — everything happens for a reason,' says Mike.

'Do you fancy her?' asks Sally.

'Irish poets do have a certain romantic charm when they are decked out in large sexy dungarees hiding their curves and rainbow crocs.'

'Why, is she a big unit?'

'I cannot comment.'

'Is she my age?'

'Never asked.'

'Children?'

'Three.'

'Boys or girls?'

'Never asked.'

'Men are all the same.'

'She's a poet. Likes rhymes, alliteration and all those poet tricks. Poetry is not my bag.'

'You liked Byron the other week when I read it out loud on the cliffs. I should read out some more. Byron. Blake. Auden. Armitage. Educate your mind. Is she our Hammerhead?'

'Unlikely. Remember what Caroline Mudd said. We'll find out one way or another soon enough.'

'Women can be bastards too. They can be just as ruthless,' says Sally. 'Betty was as complicit as her husband with Lisa's abuse.'

'Sure, the Hamiltons are sad bastards with no concept of reality,' says Mike, deciding not to mention Hamilton groping his own wife in front of him and how embarrassed she looked. She wasn't complicit.

'And if there is a Simon Lord connection?'

'I'll become his patient and have a private man-to-man chat.'

'What's our end game?'

Good question. How did he picture a satisfactory conclusion? What did justice look like? Was it overturning the inquest? He could have done that with his testimony, but changing the conclusions of an inquest was a time-consuming nightmare. Was it stopping Hamilton and Lord exploiting other vulnerable girls? Or something else, something more definitive. Something that involves Charlie Cortez?

'How do you see the end?' asks Mike.

'Poetic justice. Karma, whatever you want to call it,' she says.

'Like the Brays dying in Italy,' suggests Mike, thinking they could also be an alternative source for Hammerhead's sexploitation books.

'I told you to forget the Brays. Sod their souls,' says Sally.

'You have a point. Sod Stevie Gannon too,' says Mike, an image of his decapitated buddy flashing in and out of his mind in a microsecond.

'Who is he?'

'A fellow stuntman in America. Had an accident when he fell asleep on a railway track drunk.'

'How awful.'

'It was.'

'Would serve Hamilton and Lord right if they were guilty. An interventionist God doing some good,' says Sally.

'That's what the Pettys believe.'

Sally puffs out her cheeks and looks in her small rucksack and produces two KitKats, hands one to Mike and keeps one for herself.

'Is it worth it?' she asks him. 'What if there are no links and I am just an anxious woman misreading book porn as my best friend's confession?'

'You're a very brave woman. Took guts to say what you said at the inquest. Everyone else, me included, wanted the easiest solution that let us all off the hook. Lisa didn't kill herself so there's no way we can shoulder any blame. You were our conscience.'

'That's good of you to say that. Makes me feel less foolish,' says Sally.

'Any joy linking the other Hammerhead books to victims?'

'It's an almost impossible task. Women speak to us in confidence. I cannot betray their trust, even if it's only to you. I will keep searching, but don't have any great expectations about what I can deliver.'

'Fair enough,' says Mike.

'I could do with another drink. This whole Lisa business is exhausting me. Half a beer doesn't hit the right spots. One thing will.'

'If we open a bottle at home, you might have to stay over.'

'I thought you'd never ask. I brought my own toothbrush and clean knickers. And my white tee shirt. See if you pass the WT test.'

'I've made Angelina's bed for you. Fresh sheets.'

'Spoilsport.'

'I've got a busy day tomorrow. What are you going to text Ian? Will he be getting jealous?'

'The truth. Staying with a friend because I've drunk too much and I've let me hair down and I am off work tomorrow,' says Sally. She stands up, adjusts her dress and walks to his other less attractive side, and kneels-down, knees dimpling the sand. 'You're a good man. The kindest man I've ever met.' Runs her hand down the scars on the left-hand side of his face. Leans over and kisses his scars gently, once, twice, three times. 'I am glad you're my friend.'

If only she knew the truth about the uncut Mike Nicholls, his sins always standing in the shadows, humming.

Two texts come from both Hamiltons at the same time. He shows them to Sally. She grins and looks like Lisa in the semi-light.

Looking forward to run, run, running day after tomorrow. Shannon xxx

Are we running into our unknown....? Robin

'What do they mean?' asks Sally.

'You know what these literature types are like. Talking in riddles. If you've got the day off, you might want to come with me to Duns. You can pretend to be my occasional girlfriend, help restrain Hamilton's smutty potty mouth and his wife hitting on me,' says Mike.

'So, there are limits to what you'll do to find the truth, like sleeping with the enemy?'

'Shall we go,' he says, refusing to respond.

'No, let's snuggle up and watch the sun go down. Listen to the sound of the waves. I'll enjoy what I can of you while you're here.'

And they do. Pulling the rug around their shoulders and snuggling up together for extra warmth. He looks at her, head resting on his chest, hair falling over her face. She's fallen asleep. He'll wake her in a bit. He focuses on the fire slowly burning itself out. His hand strokes her thigh gently and he knows it is time.

'Are you awake?'

'I was drifting, miles away. Carry on. It was nice. A bit low, but nice.'

'You need to know why we are never going to happen. First, you're married. And second, I am damaged goods. Like Lisa.'

'What do you mean?'

'You deserve better than me.'

She shifts her position slightly so she can see his face. His hand still on her thigh, no longer moving.

'Stevie Gannon was my stunt co-ordinator on a film I was shooting. A larger-than-life character who liked to drink and fuck, had a big dick the size of cucumber.'

'Nice. Size isn't everything. What was the film?'

'I cannot tell you the name of the film because of a non-disclosure agreement. If I break it, they can sue for the compensation and take every penny I've earned and saved,' says Mike, thinking she thinks he's been damaged downstairs.

'You're joking. A tough Marine scared of a piece of paper.'

'I am being serious. It was a lot of money.'

'How much?'

'You're a cheeky madam. I'll tell you when you let me finish my story without interrupting with your asides.'

'Sorry. This must be hard for you.'

There she goes again with the innuendo. She cannot help herself.

'Not really. We're doing a car scene, and I am ready to go and waiting for the signal but he's looking at his mobile phone and ignoring me. Somebody must have cancelled the stunt, and I am waiting for them to tell me on the radio to abort. I don't know what to do. Then Gannon remembers and raises his hand and shouts go ... and that's the last thing I remember...'

Sally strokes the scared top of his hand on her thigh and grasps his finger.

I have no memory of what happened. I was two seconds out for the stunt timings and crashed the car and it caught fire when the petrol tank exploded. I would have burned alive, but a runner called Emile Perez unclipped my safety harnesses and pulled me free. I owe the runner my life and can never thank him enough.

Looking back, I have no emotions or memories about the accident, almost like what happened didn't really involve me. I was acting, playing a part. Like I did in war zones when we were killing people on automatic pilot like we'd been trained to do since the age of seventeen.

I was disappearing into a big black hole like they have in space, dying. Those black holes with their dark matter suck things in and nobody can escape. One minute, drunken big Steve Gannon is telling me to GO and next I am lying in a bed waiting to fall into that big black hole for infinity.

I was detached, partly because of the painkillers and the morphine and partly because of my nature. Gannon was waiting for me to die because nobody expects me to survive. I find out later Gannon never told my family about the accident. Not that I was thinking about anything other than death. I was and always will be a Marine, death is in the job description. Same as being a stunt man. It's well paid because it's dangerous and sensible people avoid risk like the plague. My death is no big news, except for mum and dad and my sister Angelina and everyone in Berwick who know me and think I am successful.

Gannon talked to me when I was too far gone to respond, but he tells me he's my best friend and he'll look after everyone and he's sorry, my timing was wrong. He should have picked a more experienced guy. I should have been paying attention.

A studio executive called David Logan comes in and asks Gannon how the patient is doing. Logan doesn't even know my name. Gannon says I'll be lucky to survive the next 24 hours.

The exec says if the stunt man pulls through Gannon needs to hush the accident up and pay me off, make me sign a non-disclosure agreement. The film's cursed enough already without a freelancer's death adding to the PR catastrophe.

Much to Gannon's surprise, after four days in intensive care, it emerges I am not going to be dying anytime soon. They won't be getting to burn the rest of me in a crematorium, throwing my ashes off a cliff into the North Sea.

Gannon's sat there telling me to forget about the doctors, the reality is going to be shit. I'll never get laid again. Serious damage has been done to my lungs and body because of my piss-poor preparation and lack of concentration. I wasn't paying attention to Gannon, because I don't care. As a result of my carelessness, I am an ex-stuntman without a face, raw flesh with frog eyes bulging out, like a fucking weird translucent fish three miles under the Pacific Ocean. Without a face, I'd never be allowed on a film set again or in a public space. Kids would cry when they saw me. Girls would run a mile. People will recognise my voice and gestures and not my face. Gannon was putting forward a convincing argument for me not hanging around.

Of course the fucker was lying to me because he has his own agenda. If I die, he was off the hook. Nobody would care. I am expendable. Brit stuntmen, ten a penny. All these insane military vets looking for thrills to chill the kill games constantly playing in their heads. That's why I can't inflict myself on Sally. I am an accident waiting to happen. Gannon wasn't alone in stitching me up. The roughs showing the accident were edited to make it my fault. When I first saw them, I believed the fake film, until Emile Perez said he'd seen the accident and they had covered it up. Everything else was destroyed. I'd never be able to prove anything. They'd all signed NDAs like I had. Apart from Emile. He was told his visa had run out and he had to go back to Mexico or be forcibly deported by ICE.

When I signed the NDA, they transferred a million dollars into my account ten minutes later and said they would pay reasonable medical bills to make me a pretty boy again. Told me if I broke the agreement, ever, they'd take all the money and everything else I owned. My life — and my family's —would be ruined beyond my imagination. I wasn't sure who was worse. Gannon or Logan.

Once the money was in my account, I took control of my emotions. There was no real point in having a complex about losing half my face. I could take a good look at myself in the mirror and see the new improved Mike Nicholls. That's who I was now, and if people don't like me, fuck them. I was not shy or embarrassed by how I looked. I wasn't a pussy covering my scalp with wigs and hats to avoid scaring people off with half an ear. No big deal. Holyfield survived Tyson's ring cannibalism. Wears his wounds with pride

My burns were superficial injuries. An eye surgeon took skin from behind my ear to create new eyelids. His colleague and business partner in his clinic said he would take a bit of rib cartridge and build me a new ear, take hair from the back of my head and fix my eyebrows. Bum hair would fix my bald patch. I told them I was a Marine first and foremost and a pretty boy second. My mates suffered far worse than me. Dead. Limbless. Brain damaged and there was big Mike Nicholls crying over a few burns.

The fire is almost out. The blood red sky has faded from view. They are
shivering underneath the rug. She lifts his hand and presses it into the
middle of her chest.

'Thank you for telling me,' says Sally.

'What happened to Gannon?'

'A Kentucky rail freight train finished his story.'

'Meaning?'

'He had an accident. Fell asleep drunk on a train track and a freight
train ripped his head and legs off him. They found his legs a quarter of a
mile down the track.'

'Karma?'

'You could say that,' says Mike, stopping the story short, the punchline
protected by a metaphorical NDA signed by him and Charlie Cortez.

Sally, still holding Mike's hand, fingers splayed, to her chest, says he
must feel exhausted after that conversation. It was tough listening for
her, but much worse for him. She thanks him for placing his faith in her
as a confidant and she will never tell anyone what's he just said.

'You ever told anyone else?'

'Only one person, two actually.'

'Who?'

'You know one. The other is my sister. They understand pain.'

'More than me? And you?'

'Hopefully yes. Let's avoid getting sentimental. Tomorrow, we seduce
the Hamiltons,' says Mike.

'You mean make us interesting, irresistible and intriguing — or do
you mean literally?' asks Sally.

10

Next morning they are standing in a square facing each other on the Hamilton's patio. They are ready and waiting for the fun to begin when Mike puts them through their paces. The Hamilton's kids are at a private school outside of Berwick, an hour's round trip twice a day for Shannon. The sun is shining, and the sky is blue and the wind less intense than on the coast.

Mike's wearing a black second skin, a Tom Cruise as *Jack Reacher* baseball cap, an *Inglourious Basterds* black tee shirt featuring Brad Pitt on the front, black shorts, black socks, black tights and black trainers. Sally has borrowed his sister Angelina's gym kit and looks like she's been spray painted in black. Shannon is wearing floral jogging pants and a body conscious baggy top. Hamilton is dressed for a Manchester nineties rave, baggy shorts, brightly flowered top, grey socks and green outsized trainers.

'I've not done this since I had sessions in LA with Tom and Katie and George and Amal back in the day, although that's strictly off the record. What happens in LA with Cruisey and the Cloons stays in LA. I've got great stories, but I value their friendship more.'

'You know them personally?' asks Shannon.

'Their personal mobile numbers are in my phone. Tom got me my first stunt job in *Jack*. Worked with George on *The American*. And *The*

Monuments Men. That's hush, hush. Strictly confidential. We exchange Xmas cards.'

Mike introduces Sally, an exercise buddy staying at his as she has a couple of days off from the domestic abuse unit where she supports sex assault victims to rebuild their lives. He asks the Hamiltons when they last did any serious organised training.

'Fifty years ago, when I was at boarding school. Not done anything since, apart from my right hand, drinking beer and wine and cider and obviously my right hand is my wa...' says Hamilton.

Shannon interrupts him and tells him to behave himself. They have guests. Says she did lots of sports at Uni and ran in her teens. Kids mean she has less time to workout than she would like.

Mike says his aim isn't to turn them into Tom Cruise and Nicole Kidman overnight but to kickstart a healthier lifestyle for them. He says it's about starting with the basics. Moving the body every single day, avoiding sedentary behaviour, difficult for writers. There are three objectives. Cardio, keeping the heart rate up, the second is strength training, push-ups, and squats, and lunges, and third is flexibility and making sure that everything is stretched.

He drops down and does twenty press ups, says they must find the right exercise dosage for them and make sure they are motivated to get fit and stay fit.

'Am I doing press ups or running?' asks Hamilton, jogging on the spot and doing mock stand-up press-ups, pushing against fresh air like Trump mocking a journalist with disabilities.

'At the moment you're making a fool of yourself, wasting my time,' says Mike, like he's back at marine training school in Lympstone, Devon.

'Nobody's spoken to me like that since boarding school,' says Hamilton. 'Did you speak to Tom and George like that?'

'Yes, and worse. They respected me for it.'

Two hours later, they are back on the patio, Shannon's serving lunch on a bench and an unfit red-faced Hamilton is necking pints of water, towel around his neck, large sweat stains under his arms.

Sally's helping Shannon in the kitchen and has left Lisa's copy of *Angel Face* on an oak coffee table in the open plan living room, their version of a domestic IED.

Mike wanders over to Hamilton. He's barely broken sweat, but they've *bonded*.

'Enjoy yourself?'

'Hard work. Sally is a spit for Nicole Kidman. Are you giving her one?'

'What happens in Berwick...'

'...stays in Berwick, I get the gist. But it doesn't have to be like that.'

'What do you mean?'

'You must have a ton of stories to tell about film stars and directors you've worked with. Tom. George. Brad. We should team up. Put all your stories on tape and I'll write them up and disguise them, so we avoid going to court. A fifty-forty deal, your ideas, my writing skills, with the spare ten for my agent, Lucy.'

'Forty for who? You?'

'I am not only the greatest living satirist in England, I am also the most discreet ghostwriter too.'

'Why are you worth fifty?'

'No disrespect, you're anonymous, invisible. But you won't be once you hook up with Lucy, my literary agent. She's fantastic, ruthless, a brilliant woman and a stunning publisher.'

'What are you talking about?'

'A modern take on Kenny Anger's *Hollywood Babylon*, tall stories of sex, drugs, murder, scandal, old movies and glamorous lives. Hollywood's depravity rebooted by Brit war hero and courageous stuntman Michael D Nicholls...what's not to like. It's all totally outrageous and libellous, ridiculously fake, but it will shift ...'

'Any examples of similar books?'

'Not any that involve me.'

'A great idea, but reliving that period in my life is too painful, the accident is too traumatic,' says Mike.

'I've googled you. No mention of an accident.'

'I signed an NDA, and they disappeared me and the car crash. I really should get counselling, but there's nobody I can trust. There's so much on my mind. The crash. The wars in Iraq and Afghanistan. My grandfather was in Berlin after the second world war and talked about the Russians raping woman and girls on an industrial scale, treating them as sexual spoils of war. I saw too many Brit soldiers do the same,' says Mike.

'How awful!'

'I need to tell someone. Get it out of my head.'

'Tell me. I am a good and discreet listener,' says Hamilton.

'No offence, but I need a professional. Unlocking the mind is very dangerous. I'd hate to have a breakdown...I am hanging on.'

'I can help you.'

'The stories in my head...'

'I have a friend, a counsellor...his name is...'

Shannon interrupts Hamilton, storming out of the house and throwing a book at his face and hitting him. Mike's impressed by her accuracy, but not her timing.

'What's this fucking filth doing in my house where my kids might pick it up. I don't want their minds perverted with unnatural acts.'

'Christ, Shannon,' exclaims Hamilton, his nose dripping blood onto his chin.

'What's up?' asks Mike, feigning confusion.

Shannon stomps over to where Mike and Hamilton are talking, picks up the book and slaps her husband around the head, cursing him as each blow lands. She throws the book to the ground.

'This filth is not allowed near our kids, how many times do you have to be told.'

Hamilton hides behind Mike, creating a barrier between his furious wife and himself.

'I've not brought any filthy book in the house, darling. Calm down, you're embarrassing yourself.'

On cue, Sally comes out of the house, asking if anyone's seen her book, must have fallen out of her bag when she went to the loo.

'What's it called?' asks Shannon.

'*Angel Face*,' replies Sally.

'This yours?'

'I've not started it yet. A friend lent to me. Said it was saucy. Would spice up my love life,' says Sally.

'I told you sweetie,' says Hamilton. 'Nothing to do with me. It's Sally's book. Just a coincidence.'

'Are you two OK?' asks Mike, picking up the book. 'J.D.Hammerhead? Never heard of him. What's the book about?'

'Molestation and child abuse,' says Shannon, before Hamilton can interrupt her.

'It's a harmless book of sexual fantasies. We're all adults with needs. A friend left a copy ages ago. One of the kids picked it up. That's why my sweetheart is annoyed, isn't it love?'

'If you say so,' says Shannon, her anger dissipating as she watches Hamilton wipe up the blood with his hanky, leaning his head back to stem the flow. 'I have warned you so many times.'

'Money, money, money,' asks Hamilton, staring hard at his wife, oblivious to Sally and Mike. 'You want your cake, and you want to eat it, and then you wonder why you bloody put so much weight on.'

Mike is tempted to read out a passage from *Angel Face* to distract Hamilton from bullying his wife. Rub his nose in the pile of shit he's denies creating, but who knows what's going to happen next.

'Not sure I should be reading a book about molestation and child abuse. Have you read it Shannon...?' asks Sally, innocently.

'I read all my husband's...' Shannon stops before ending the sentence, green eyes ready to overflow. 'I'd chuck it in the bin, Sally, you look like a nice girl. I enjoyed training with you.'

'Sally won't be here next time. She's got lives to save, but are we OK day after tomorrow? Same time,' says Mike. 'If you can give me the name of your counsellor, that would be great.

Mike and Sally don't say a word as her red Audi races through the country lanes back towards Berwick. Finally, she breaks the silence when they are clear of Duns.

'Your bloody plan worked. We're barking up the right tree.'

'Did you get her mobile?'

'Yes. She damn near broke his nose. Blood everywhere.'

'Brilliant work from your end. Timing slightly off, but I'd take it. He pitched me a ghost-writing gig too, same deal as *Angel Face* I would imagine. He's going to introduce me to his counsellor, and I'd bet my house that it's Simon Lord,' says Mike.

'He's definitely guilty, and she needs an exit plan fast,' replies Sally. 'They have an abusive, coercive relationship.'

'Like you do with Ian?'

'Ian's just a nob who can't get it up. Blames me for exerting too much pressure on him to perform. My fault for not doing anything. If Shannon reaches out to me, it stays private between me and her. You understand?'

Mike nods, he would never have it any other way. Hamilton was an odious creature, protected by the establishment because he is one of them. Splitting up his marriage to Shannon is a good thing, protecting her, the kids and Patch, the dog.

Was it enough? Not really. Hamilton, like Boris Johnson or Elon Musk, would simply find another younger trophy wife and father more sprogs. Hamilton needed to know he'd done wrong and feel the pain.

When they arrive in Berwick, they check their mobiles.

A text arrives from Hamilton to Mike: *grt work out 2day. Sorry abt S. Menopause. My c'sor mt is Simon Lord. Spk to him and he says get in touch. He has cancellation 2morrow. Send contact details sep text. See u day after 2tomrrow. Rob.*

Another one: *will pray 2 God 2 lead you where he wants.*

Finally, the contact details for Simon Lord, mobile, email and two addresses, one in Morpeth and another in Alnwick.

And from Shannon to Sally: *so sorry you saw that today. Throw that book away. It's evil like the bastard who wrote it and calls it sexual satire in the spirit of Anais Nin. He disgusts me. Goodnight. Love Shaz xx*

He calls Simon Lord immediately and leaves a message: *my name is Mike Nicholls. My good friend Robin Hamilton recommended you as a counsellor who can help me cope with severe violent and sexual trauma.*

Still not speaking, they get out of the red Audi and Mike nods towards the cliffs on the other side of the estuary several miles away. Time to do a proper workout and give them a bit of relief from the sleaze. They both feel contaminated by their proximity to a sexual predator disguised as a country toff and need power-hosing down.

'If you try and overtake on the cliffs, do it on the right-hand side,' says Mike. Charlie Cortez would have laughed at his black humour for all the wrong reasons, same as seeing a colleague have his lower legs blown off when he stepped on an IED in Afghanistan. He'd screamed he'd lost his legs, and Charlie would say under his breath, they were over there, should have watched where he was walking. Same as Big Stevie Gannon after the 04.35 passed over him. Charlie was like that; pragmatism ran through him like the lettering on a stick of Blackpool rock.

Before they set off on their run, a text comes through from Simon Lord: *I've got a cancellation tomorrow. Alnwick 11.00? RSVP first come, first served. Confirm ASAP. Session £120 upfront. Follow link on next text. Si.*

Bingo, says Mike to himself, he can meet Simon Lord face-to-face and uncover a few home truths.

11

Simon Lord recognises him when Mike steps into the open reception of his offices in the small market town of Alnwick in Northumberland, thirty odd miles down the A1 from Berwick. The office space is shared with a financial advisor, a surveyor, a conveyor, a communications consultant, social media expert and a physiotherapist, according to the names on the front door.

'Aren't you Lisa's friend from the inquest? You're...,' says Lord, motioning to his own head and drawing his own scars with his fingers, '...the man in the toilet?'

'Callum stumbled on a slippery floor. Pure coincidence I am here. I only bumped into Robin Hamilton a few days ago after crashing into his rear. Never met him before, but I love his books. All of them. He thoroughly endorsed you. Is it a problem?'

'Of course not,' says Lord. 'You've paid for the exploratory session to see if I think I can help you.'

'It was Robin's idea. I am old school. Seeking help is a sign of weakness,' says Mike.

'We're here to chat, not pass judgement. Relax and make yourself at home. Coffee, tea, water?'

Mike shakes his head, says he only has coffee first thing in the morning to clear the fog from his brain. Only drinks tea when he's fighting wars and killing brown people. He laughs too loudly and then sits on his hands like a naughty schoolboy, looking for an opportunity to strike at the counsellor's defences. He knows he's intimidated by violence, like most people. Elbowing Callum Petty in the face by mistake was a good advert for him.

'An army joke?'

'No, I am a former Marine. Not a pongo.'

'Is there a difference?'

'Probably not,' says Mike, the counsellor looks far less comfortable than at the inquest. Being alone in a room with a man pretending to be a psychopath tends to make reasonable people edgy.

Simon races through his ground rules, explains they need a written agreement to cover confidentiality, boundaries, time-keeping, appointments, note-taking and anything else deemed to be relevant. Once they've finished the sessions, the contract is destroyed, and his case notes are safely locked away for seven years and then they too are destroyed.

'Is this the admin stuff in case of a car crash?'

'One way of looking at it, I suppose.'

'Nothing is taped?'

'Of course not, unless you want to record your sessions.'

'Why would I want to do that? If anyone knew what happened to me, I'd never live it down,' says Mike.

'There is absolutely no taping.'

'I can read the notes you write about me?'

'Absolutely anytime.'

'Strictly confidential between you and me?'

Lord says there's an uninvited guest who has taken permanent residence in Mike's head and is eating him up bit by bit, cell by cell, atom by atom, starving him of any future happiness and hope. His enemy is a cancer that thinks it can give chemo, radiation and surgery the middle finger, confident it cannot be destroyed. They can beat it. Dr Simon Lord and Mike Nicholls, once he opens-up. How did that sound?

'Sounds just what the doctor ordered,' says Mike. Had Lisa fallen for the snake oil sales pitch to village idiots? Was that why she opened up to him?

'In my experience, the sooner survivors of sexual violence talk the better. My professional advice is you might as well get it off your chest right now. Free those bad memories trapped inside here,' Simon says, tapping the side of his head.

'Trapped in here, right on,' says Mike, tapping hard on his own skull.

'We can, this minute, Mike Nicholls. Your recovery begins here. Don't worry, your counselling is one hundred percent private and one hundred percent confidential. You're not feeling suicidal are you, or wanting to hurt yourself?'

'I am scared of what might happen if we start digging. I am afraid that certain things are buried too deep.'

'Don't be ashamed of being afraid. Remembering and re-living your sexual abuse experience is the crucial first step. We must take it before we start trauma recovery counselling. Only then can we give you practical tools and techniques to process what has happened, repair and build your self-esteem and improve your coping mechanisms.'

'Will you help me stop wanting to hurt myself?'

'Of course, with my help, shocking memories that were once powerful will cease to trigger such intense emotions and will no longer be barriers to you living a rewarding and happy life.'

'Sure sounds impressive,' says Mike. 'I like the cut of your jib.'

'Thank you, but to be honest, I know nothing about you. No medical files. Just a recommendation from a very good friend. Do you belong to the Brotherhood as well? That's where me and Robin met. Callum and Susan are an amazing couple. Their belief in God is absolute. Never any doubt.'

'No, my only brotherhood is the green beret brigade, welcome anywhere in the world.'

'Do you want to tell me what's troubling you?'

'It's about Lisa.'

'I thought we were going to talk about you. I can't talk about clients,' says Lord.

'Even dead ones?'

'Robin said killing and rape in war zones are heavy on your mind. Did you really work with those film stars he mentioned, Tom and Nicole, Brad and George?'

'Killing people and raping people is more Charlie Cortez territory than mine.'

'Who is Charlie Cortez?'

'Your worst nightmare,' says Mike.

'I am not understanding you,' says the counsellor.

'Lisa's death triggered nasty thoughts inside my head. She was raped multiple times by people she trusted and was raped again when you and Hamilton published this piece of shit novel.'

Mike takes the book from his man bag and offers it to Simon Lord, who glances at the cover and quickly looks away again.

'*Angel Face*? That book is nothing to do with me?'

'Not what I've been told.'

'I think you should leave, now. I'll refund you your money. I won't be intimidated by you.'

'Your friend Robin Hamilton wrote it, calls himself J.D.Hammerhead.'

'How does that involve me?'

Mike gives him the steady unblinking cold eyes and knows his stare can make certain kind of men like the counsellor go weak at the knees and piss themselves.

'Let's see. You gave her the spiel you just gave me. You secretly taped the conversation, and you gave the transcript to Robin Hamilton. This is the result,' says Mike, thrusting the book towards the counsellor, who raises his hands in surrender. Mike knows he can only use this tactic once. He'll never catch the counsellor off-guard again without force.

'No.'

'This is book is probably why Lisa killed herself and I want the truth from you.'

'You're scaring me.'

'I've only just started. Shall I tell you about the man who did this to me?' asks Mike, pointing to his scars. Before you tell me your truth, let me tell you about Big Stevie Gannon.'

Big Stevie Gannon was the stunt co-ordinator responsible for ruining my good looks. He wasn't paying attention, called me too late and hadn't done his due diligence on the crash car stunt. He was texting on his mobile when he should have been concentrating on me. If he apologised afterwards, held up his hands and said accidents will happen, I'd have been willing to forgive him. Nobody's perfect, we all make mistakes. In a high-risk profession, they can be fatal. Doctors kill people all the time when they are operating on them. An occupational hazard. Turns out he was more interested in protecting his own skin than my burned flesh. He pinned the blame on me. On a break from the movies, he was on leave in Kentucky when he got unlucky. A junky hooker promised him the best sex ever in return for the money to buy what turned out to be her last fix. We'll call her Delores for the sake of the story. She was unlucky in Kentucky too, one bad fix too many, but that's another morning glory. Turns out Delores underestimated her Fentanyl dosage. Forget her. She was dying the day she was born. Gannon and this junky pick an isolated rail feeding depot for blow jobs and anal. You know the saying, two's company, three's a crowd? Well, Delores and Big Steve are joined by Charlie Cortez and his bottle of King of Kentucky ultra-premium straight bourbon whiskey. I am not sure if I've introduced Charlie to you, he's a good friend of mine, like the big tough brother I never had, although we are the same age. Former Marine, ginger, bit of a recluse nowadays on account of the nightmares in his head. Charlie's pissed off with Gannon on my behalf and interrupts the love making. Tells Delores to sling her hook because him and Gannon want a drink. And they do, except Charlie's teetotal on account of the voices inside his head and so he lets Gannon sip the bourbon nice and slow so he doesn't throw up drinking too fast. Charlie has his double-edged marine blade underneath Gannon scrotum to make sure he doesn't spill none of that precious bourbon. The greedy pig drinks himself into a stupor and has a need to lie down to sleep it off. Silly fool falls asleep right in the middle of the track. Charlie's having a long leak, counting the stars above his head when a train rides right over Big Steve. Lops off his head and his lower legs. Imagine a massive blade chopping you in two, like a guillotine.

'I've got a picture of Big Steve's head and shoulders on my phone. You want to see it?'

'No.'

'Tell me what you know about Lisa, her abuse and *Angel Face?*'

'And then you'll leave?'

'If you convince me you're telling me the truth, I'll be on my way.'

Simon Lord looks beaten, ready to do anything to stop the nightmare in front of him.

'I already knew Lisa's abuse before I ever met her.'

'How come?'

'What the hell. They are dead. You swear this is strictly confidential?'

'You have my word,' says Mike.

'Why should I trust you?'

'Look at this.'

I show Lord the image of Big Stevie Gannon's drunken head and shoulders, the red MAGA baseball cap lodged tight on his forehead, hiding his receding, thinning flaxen mullet. I show another pic. A selfie with the photographer bending down, using Gannon's head as a pillow. I say the man with Stevie is wearing a Marine-issue Kestrel helmet-mounted night vision system and binocular night vision system and an ops-core helmet, the high cut shell providing protection from blunt trauma forces. He's donning a ballistic-facemask made from bullet resistant material with the inside padded for shock absorption.

'That's my confession. Now give me yours,' says Mike, unsure if he's just scared Lord into traumatic silence. 'Lisa and this book? What's the story?'

'Robin told me,' says Lord, a look of total resignation etched across his face.

'When?'

'I cannot betray a trust.'

'Just let the words flow. It's easy to free your conscience,' says Mike. 'Tell me about Hammerhead aka Robin Hamilton and how he knew about Lisa's abuse?'

'Robin's been a client for many years. He's confused about everything. His sexuality. Finances. Self-esteem. Body image. You name it, it worries him, but go easy on him. He writes those books for money because he's skint. Says his mother never loved him as a child.'

'Lisa's abuse?'

'Robin said he had a party at his house several years ago and somebody discussed sexual fantasies, said there was money in erotica.'

'Who?'

'He never said.'

'You weren't there?'

'No, after the success of the book, he would spend our sessions telling me he was hungry for real life sex stories.'

'And did you feed him more stories told to you in good faith from abused women? He's written more books after *Angel Face!* Don't answer. You're not going to do it again are you?'

'Never again, I am so sorry.'

Lord pauses for a second or two, says if Mike wants real help, he can recommend somebody to help him come to terms with his violence.

'And what have I done?' asks Mike.

'You are a killer, you've got the same haunted eyes as Lisa and Sally. Maybe that's why you all have a natural affinity for each other. Whether your Charlie Cortez story is true or not, I saw you and Sally at the inquest. Irresistibly drawn to each other like moths to a light, like a couple of lemmings..,' says Lord.

'...ready to jump off cliffs? That's insensitive.'

'That's a myth. Lemmings can swim. If they reach a water obstacle, such as a river or lake, they may try to cross it. Inevitably, a few individuals drown. But it's hardly suicide.'

'Your sessions with Lisa?

'She laughed at me. Said she was only here to keep her mate Sally happy. Said Sally was upset she had betrayed her and was sat outside in her car. Lisa doesn't drive and Sally does. Said I was to tell everyone we had great sessions, keep Sally placated. Her friendship was the most important thing in the world to her.'

'Then what did you do?'

'Read books and sipped wine for four weeks during our sessions, until she got bored and stopped coming. Or Sally stopped offering her lifts. One or the other.'

'If you tell anyone about this conversation, I'll be back with Charlie. That's a promise.'

12

Mike has a lot to think about and wakes at six in the morning. Fifteen minutes later, after a coffee and a bagel, he's running hard through Berwick town centre and across the old bridge towards the cliffs to Cocklawburn. He needs to replay the events since the inquest until they make sense and give him a path to follow.

Simon Lord is a dead end, if he believes him, and there is no reason why he shouldn't. His version of events didn't sound rehearsed and his fear was palpable. If it's true and weak Simon Lord is out of the frame, Sally, Lisa and the Brays are in the dock.

And why is Sally lying about her friendship with Lisa? She is adamant they were estranged, testified at the inquest that they had fallen out. He could call Sally now and ask her direct, except her answer will disappoint him. Has she been flirting with him so he takes his eye off the ball? Why is she trying to distract him? Did she send Lisa the book? Why else would Lisa be reading such filth?

The harder he runs, the more confused he becomes until it stops making any sense at all.

Showered and shaved with freshly washed PT kit on minus the Hollywood heroes on his tee, he's driving to Duns through the county lanes, chilling out and listening to Joe Strummer's epic 17-minute *Minstrel Boy* from his *Global a Go-Go* album.

A driver races up behind him in his rear-view mirror travelling well over seventy miles per hour. Count to ten. Fat chance. He gets to four and the red Audi overtakes and is gone, oblivious to what might be coming around the bend.

'Twat.'

Was that Sally? She is back at work in A&E unless she's taken another day off. She would not be that reckless. Nurses deal with the consequences of speeding careless drivers. They don't cause the accidents themselves.

Turning right onto the A661 into Duns, he finds himself stuck behind a sedate blue Range Rover with a Brotherhood of Jesus sticker in the back window. He ends up following it into Hamilton's drive, almost bumping into the red Audi.

A riot's taking place on the patio. Three adults are gesturing, shouting and pointing at each other. Quick as a flash, Mike is out of his car. Hamilton's pleading with his wife who is being held by Sally in her nurse's uniform.

'I'll change. I swear to God I'll change. I'll become the man you want me to be. Please don't go. Please don't leave me this way,' cries Hamilton, his voice swamped in self-pity.

'Always promises. Empty promises. I cannot believe you are swearing to God you'll change. How many times,' says Shannon, calm as a cucumber, in stark contrast to the blubbering satirist dressed in baggy shorts and a vest.

Hamilton drops slowly to his knees and begs, like he's pleading for his life. He's directly in front of Shannon and a uniformed Sally steps between them. Callum and Susan Petty join them, the head of the Brotherhood's voice telling everyone to calm down.

'I warned you about those books. Money is not important. We don't need this house. We don't need these riches for a good life,' says Shannon.

'What's going on?' asks Mike. 'What are you doing here, Sally?'

'Look at Shannon's face.'

Mike does. Shannon's been hit.

'Who?'

'Him,' Sally and Shannon reply at the same time, pointing at the badly dressed satirist.

'I am sorry, my fist slipped. Everyone deserves a second chance, everyone deserves a second chance,' responds Hamilton.

'Like Ricky Hatton hitting Floyd Mayweather Jr. with his face until he knocked himself out,' says Mike, flexing his shoulders and crunching his fists.

'How many chances have you had? Two or three. Fifty more like. Always the same. Promise to change but like an alcoholic, you cannot stop yourself sliding into bad habits,' says Shannon.

'I think you two need to back off and give this loving couple room to breathe,' says Callum.

'Shannon called asking for my help. I am not leaving this courtyard without her and the kids,' says Sally.

'They are at school,' cries Hamilton.

'Susan, can you...,' says Callum.

'...do nothing. It's not your business,' says Mike.

'...And it's none of your business, Action Man. Stop trying to play the big macho hero, a third-rate *Jack Reacher*. Stop rocking the boat and trying to destroy his family,' says Callum.

'He's done a pretty good job without my assistance,' says Mike.

Petty shrugs his shoulders and says it is not worth falling out over a bloody sex book for masturbating unbelievers.

'If you don't like it, don't pick it up.'

Mike thinks about asking if the same applies to the bible and interpreting it to suit your lifestyle, but he's too busy staring Petty down, who, unlike Hamilton, is not intimidated one iota by the former Marine.

'What you describe in those books is horrible and to say that they enjoy it is even worse. How can you possibly do that?' asks Mike.

'My mother never wanted me. Wished I'd been a girl. How are you meant to cope with that? Satire was my only escape from my domineering mum.'

'Your mother's been dead ten years,' says Shannon.

'She still haunts me.'

'That why you belted me, because your mother never loved you? Grow up, spoilt child,' says Shannon.

Callum says everyone should take ten seconds to pause and let the anger subside, offer the Lord a prayer, ask for his forgiveness. If they pray together the message will be stronger and quicker.

He clasps his hands together.

'Dear Lord, please forgive our brother and sister, Robin and Shannon, and please ask Michael and Sally to understand a man and her wife have obligations to each other and no one should interfere with their duties. Amen.'

'Thank you, Callum,' says Hamilton.

'Now unpack and get yourself back in the house and looking after your husband and your children and the Brotherhood,' says Callum.

'I rejected Catholicism and was baptised into the Brotherhood for you, but you treat me like a doormat, constantly walking over me. You think you're funny and clever, but I'll kill you or jump off a cliff,' says Shannon.

'Sob, sob,' says Hamilton, seemingly reinvigorated after Callum's intervention with prayer.

Callum walks up to Mike and whispers into his good ear that Robin just needs time to get things sorted out with his wife. Maybe him and Sally could go and book a hotel room for a couple of hours and work off their excessive energy by fucking each stupid like unbelievers do. Come back when everything is resolved. Mike laughs at him and shakes his head. He can hear Charlie Cortez whispering in his left half ear: *deck him out cold, the cunt.*

'Leave this to me, Mike. Callum, no disrespect, but nothing's going to stop me helping Shannon, including you two,' says Sally.

'You're getting over-emotional, like you did at the bloody inquest,' says Callum.

Sally takes out her mobile and Mike sees her pressing the screen rapidly several times.

'We're about to go live on social media showing this pathetic man crying on the patio and his wife sporting a black eye after being punched in the face with his fist. What will the world think of Britain's greatest living satirist?'

'You're bluffing,' says Callum.

'Try me,' says Sally.

Callum turns to Mike.

'Keep your bitch under control.'

'The apple doesn't fall far from the tree does it,' says Sally. 'You knew about Lisa's abuse and did nothing.'

'We have laws within the Brotherhood, and she broke and disrespected them when she had relationships outside of our community.'

'She was groomed and raped by adults who were meant to be looking after her welfare. Are you blinded by your religion?'

'Like me. Him putting his hand up my skirt and fingering me and his friends just watching and laughing while I'm being humiliated,' says Shannon.

'You owe me. I gave you attention and credibility when you weren't even famous as a poet in your own Dublin living room. I got you an agent Lucy Graham and she helped build your career and you want to walk away from me? Lucy will sack you.'

'Too late, mate, Lucy will be calling you soon saying she can no longer represent you as there are complaints about your behaviour from your wife and your wife is also one of her clients and she can't accept the conflict of interest...,' says Shannon.

Nobody's listening to her, everybody is watching Hamilton go from begging on his knees to lying on his back, clutching his chest, his face like Caravaggio's *Medusa*.

Mike's thinking Hamilton is either play-acting or having a heart attack. Sally knows it is the latter because she is calling 999.

Not another bloody inquest, he'll need a season ticket as he watches Sally rush over to England's greatest living satirist and asks everyone to give her room as she is about to start CPR.

Mike whispers under his breath to nobody, don't die. There are too many unanswered questions. If Hamilton pegs it, how is he going to find out who gave him the *Angel Face* story.

13

While the by-standers gawp, feet frozen to the patio paving stones, Mike takes the mobile from Sally and speaks to the emergency services, giving them their exact location and details about the writer's current state of poor health. He tells the operator an A&E nurse is on the scene, but they still need an ambulance and paramedics ASAP.

The operator asks if the nurse needs help and Mike says everything appears to be under control, but the golden hour is already ticking down. They need to get their skates on.

Is Hamilton going to die? The arguing stops, the anger replaced by a medical emergency. While Mike initially hesitates like everyone else, Sally acts to try to save the life of the man probably responsible for the death of her best friend.

Mike's impressed by her prompt intervention. Music's loss is medicine's gain as she skilfully keeps fat boy alive with methodical chest compressions and mouth-to-mouth resuscitation until the ambulance comes and takes over, blue lights flashing.

Charlie Cortez would have suggested pretending to give the writer the kiss of life, nobody would notice. Let karma ride its course. Don't inflate the lungs until the brain damage kicks in and he's left a cabbage or kicks the bucket. Charlie is like that, ruthless.

Sally stands back from Hamilton leaving him in the care of the paramedics. She collects her mobile from Mike and sidles up to him.

'How did it go with Simon Lord?'

'A blank.'

'How come.'

'She never discussed it with him. But you know that,' says Mike, whispering the last few words, unsure if she hears him in the chaos.

Sally walks away over to Shannon and hugs her and asks does she want to stay or go. Her place at the refuge is still open, nothing has changed. Shannon would have to make the decision one day, so why prolong her suffering. Better to make a clean break now and rebuild her life and cut those ties to an abusive partner.

Callum says Shannon can stay at the Brotherhood's retreat for as long as she likes and visit Robin as he recovers from his heart attack. They can prayer together to God for a reconciliation. The more they reach out, the greater the response.

Shannon is wavering, her Irish temper back under control seeing the man she must have once loved grounded.

'I should go with him,' says Shannon. 'Nobody should ever die alone.'

'Why?' asks Mike.

'None of your business, I think you and your girlfriend can leave. We'll look after our own flesh and blood,' says Callum.

'Like you did with Lisa?' asks Sally.

'Not the right time,' says Callum. 'Are you autistic as well as insensitive?'

'When is?' asks Mike.

'Please stop bickering,' says Susan Petty. 'Shall I make tea?'

The universal answer to any stressful situation, a cup of char with two sugars and a couple of rich tea biscuits.

Callum offers to help her and says he hopes he meets Mike and Sally under better circumstances. They must come and visit the Brotherhood's retreat. It's not too far away. They always welcome unbelievers if they are ready to take the pledge of allegiance to Jesus.

The paramedics have stabilised Hamilton and are explaining to Shannon what happens next. Her husband is sedated, and they are going to blue light him to the A&E at the Borders General Hospital in Melrose, about a forty-minute drive. Does she want to come with them, or will she follow in a car? Shannon looks at Sally for help and then Mike, as if to say, what should she do.

'You have to make your own mind up,' says Sally. 'What's best for you and your kids right now, this moment in time?'

'Will you come with me to the hospital?' Shannon asks Sally, who nods her assent. 'I want to make sure he's going to be OK before I decide on what to do. I'll ask Susan to collect my girls.'

Susan nods her agreement and disappears into the house to make tea that nobody is going to have time to drink. The paramedics are loading Hamilton into the ambulance.

Sally comes over again and says their hunt will be over if Hamilton dies or is left incommunicado in a permanent negative state with brain damage.

'The book is closed. I was convinced Simon Lord must have been the source,' says Sally.

'If you get a chance, ask Shannon while you're waiting at the hospital,' asks Mike, thinking Sally is quitting the hunt because she knows the answers and always did.

'Will try.'

Sally and Shannon follow the ambulance in the red Audi. The Pettys bring out tea. Susan offers Mike a cup and he accepts, and they sit down all civilised at the table dunking rich tea biscuits.

'Sorry about earlier,' says Callum. 'Those love birds always fall out.'

'Shannon doesn't like his second more lucrative career as a pornographer,' says Mike ruefully, adding the Pettys to his decreasing short-list of *Angel Face* leakers.

'Cold feet, that's her problem. Her silly Catholic conscience. Less Pope, more bible. She never really, truly embraced the Brotherhood. She was laughing with the rest of us when Robin first mentioned the idea.'

'Who was 'us'?'

'We were all sat around the table having nosh and a glass of wine and Robin was on his soap box talking about how shit the publishing world is in this country. How celebrity authors and their dodgy ghostwriters attract the marketing spend and the PR pounds while literary authors are scrapping around for pennies. He may be the greatest living English satirist, but you cannot send your kids to public school with a handful of awards. His royalties barely cover his wine bill, and he needs to find other money-making avenues,' says Callum, smiling benignly at Mike.

'Has he got a trust fund?' asks Mike, thinking this is turning into a second inquest — the unofficial off-the-record version.

'He has, but they know what he is like and control his spending. One of the guests said two things tick all the right boxes in the world of books, celebrities and sex. Somebody else said sex sells, Robin says two minutes squelching isn't going to fill three hundred pages and everyone laughed.'

'Sex does.'

'Bryan said just make it up, use your imagination and create any fantasies you want. Robin was offended and says he's a satirist, ridiculing and lampooning institutions and real people. Nothing is fictitious. Everything he writes is based in the real world. I don't fantasise, says Robin. There is more laughter, and Bryan says he'll have a private chat with them, wink, wink.'

'Bryan who?'

'Bray. He is — or was — a member of the Brotherhood with his wife Betty. He's dead now. Him and his wife. Terrible car crash.'

'The teachers Sally accused of...you know at the inquest,' says Mike, knowing Callum's just backing up Lord's confessional revelations.

'Yes, silly girl. I've known them for years. We all went to the same boarding school, Bryan, Robin and me. Would trust them with my life. Bryan was a world class musician and teacher, Robin an award-winning satirist and I run a religious retreat that puts fallen English people back on the path of righteousness and does missionary work abroad, spreading the word of the Lord.'

'So everyone knew that J.D. Hammerhead was Robin?'

'It was a big secret for the world apart from me and Susan, Bryan and Betty, Lucy and her husband, both valuable members of the Brotherhood, and Robin and Shannon.'

'Why the big secret?'

'It's embarrassing. It was a joke. A spoof. We — or Robin — were sending up pornography, satirising it, if you will and the bloody thing started a downloading sexual frenzy.'

'Sexual fantasy not your bag?'

'Strictly missionary for me and Susan. My calling is with the Lord.

You might ridicule the Brotherhood, but we do good works, and we save people as opposed to soldiers like you extinguishing rather than nourishing life.'

'That's one point of view, I suppose,' says Mike.

Susan says they were very grateful Mike had helped Lisa. She was a very lovely girl when she was young then fell under the malign influence of Sally, an unpleasant opinionated working-class sort, married into money with Ian Palmer. Says it is love, but they know better. Lisa never found love within the Brotherhood and left the family. Susan was just glad Mike was there to give her some stability before her accident. Just a great shame that he lost not only her, but also his child. Did he have other children? Has he been married before? Did he ever see them?

'What is this?' says Mike, '40 questions? I've got a few of my own. Did Lisa mention sex and the Brays?'

'Attention seeking. That's all it was. We told her it wasn't true. She was making it up. How old was she? 14 at the time? She had a conflict with the Brotherhood. Saying she was having sex outside of the Brotherhood was meant to hurt us. Relations outside the Brotherhood are strictly forbidden. Our rules were clear. Sexual relationships are limited to heterosexual marriage between baptised believers. We expect the highest moral standards. We service God, not ourselves. We have no priests, paid ministers, or elaborate churches, robes or ceremonies. We believe Jesus lives in Heaven, but will return to the earth to save us.'

'When?'

'Soon. Lisa rejected our way of life. Believers don't join the police or the armed services.'

'She's a smart woman. What's wrong with the army?'

'Everything. You kill people. They don't send you into foreign countries armed to the back teeth to hand out food parcels to starving kids. They want you to kill the children. Prolong lucrative wars. I think you should come and join us I really do. I think you're a sad man who needs help.'

Mike gets up without offering to shake the hands of the religious duo and says it's a great shame they could not have looked after her better. As her parents, she relied on them and trusted them, and they did very little to help her.

'I don't think it's what your Lord would've wanted you to do if I'm being honest.'

'Thankfully you aren't answerable to our Lord. You'll be punished for your naivety. Jesus lives in Heaven but when he returns all those who are dead but have believed and been baptised will be raised to be judged by Jesus. Those who are found worthy will live by his side forever; those who are not, or those who have not been raised, will stay dead forever.'

'Lisa stays dead.'

'Yes.'

'Me.'

'When you die. Yes. You'll stay dead.'

'You two?'

'We'll return to stand by the side Jesus as equals. He's special, we're special.'

'Good luck with that. One more thing. Did you ever like or even love Lisa?'

'Look, sonny, you're being hoodwinked by Sally and her lies. She builds up her girlfriend as this great player, but Lisa wasn't that special, as a human or a musician. Playing viola in the Great Northern Philharmonic Orchestra in Newcastle. So what? Big fish in a small bowl. If she was good, really good, she'd be playing in New York or London or Russia or Berlin with the big boys. The Brays gave her a career and Sally is just jealous she was not the chosen one. She was even less talented than Lisa.'

'I've seen videos of her. Sounds good to me.'

'I am not sure you're qualified to judge. Her music wasn't valued by her peers in the classical music profession. Same way nobody likes her personality, apart from a control freak who enjoys breaking up relationships. If you're sleeping with Sally, you'll get all you deserve.'

'You're her parents. You're meant to love Lisa unconditionally.'

'She's not one of us. You're not one of us.'

'Aren't you meant to love everyone?'

'No. We teach people how not to be Hitler.'

'And how do you do that? By acting like him?'

'Pledges. Son. We take the pledge to exist exclusively for the Brotherhood of Jesus without compromise. No to all temptations.'

'That's a tough ask. She was just a child.'

'She was our adopted daughter who rejected our way of life. But we forgive her. You should too. And stop looking for somebody to blame other than yourself. You took her on the run. Nobody else.'

'One more thing. Her stuff is stored around my house. What shall I do with it?'

'Sell it or throw it away.'

'Don't you care?'

'We're better than worldly possessions,' says Callum. 'Keep them, sell them or throw them away.'

Mike turns away and gets his car and drives off into Duns feeling filthy, like he did when fighting wars and killing people indiscriminately. He thought over time he'd forget, but he hasn't. Only Lisa gave him temporary respite before adding to his heavy load.

He needs a stiff drink or something to get rid of the anger and the frustration building inside. Like Simon Lord said, it's a cancer that will destroy him if he's not careful. He knows he needs to start the process of finally washing Lisa off his body and out of his mind. It's no good having her lodging there permanently. He's already run once today and knows as soon as he gets back to Berwick he can run again.

First, he must find out what's happened to Hamilton — has the dirty old bastard pegged it and received a one-way ticket straight to hell?

14

Mike calls Sally on the mobile and she updates him on the health and welfare of Robin C Hamilton, who has, thanks to her rapid intervention, avoided a trip to a blast furnace that never stops. The price he has paid to continue his sorry life as a satirist and pornographer is three hours of triple by-pass surgery and a long torso scar as a memento of his luckiest day.

Sally says Hamilton will have to stay in hospital for around seven days so medical staff can closely monitor his recovery. The obese outsized satirist is full of tubes, drips and drains, painkillers and anecdotes galore about his dance with death that he can commercialise. Hamilton should be able to sit in a chair after one day, walk after three days, and climb and ascend stairs by the end of the week. He can expect to make a full recovery within three months of the operation. Naturally he will feel a bit low after having bypass surgery. He'll experience good and bad days and he must realise his recovery will take weeks, rather than days. His mood won't be helped by the news that his wife and kids are about to leave him and won't be supporting him while he takes advantage of his second chance.

Sally says his agent — Lucy Graham — flew up by helicopter to handle negotiations with his estranged wife and is already releasing press statements to the media. He's newsworthy and there will be an upward spike in his sales whenever he makes the nationals for good or bad reasons. Lucy says Shannon has agreed to release a joint-statement, avoiding talk of splits and violence. Good for her sales too. Drives traffic.

'Is Shannon going to a refuge with you and her children?' asks Mike, expecting the wife to have changed her mind about exiting an unhappy marriage. Pragmatism and money always trump common sense in the end.

'No.'

'That's a shame. Bastards like him always win.'

'She wants to go to Ireland and leave her kids with here parents...and she wants me to take her. My red Audi is too small. Can you help? Driving and an intimidating presence?'

'How? Do I need to call Charlie Cortez?'

'Very funny. Get us a big enough car to transport a family from the borders to Dublin ASAP. No invite for your mate Charlie, mind.'

'Do we need passports?'

'Yes, the Irish might ask for identification. Better safe than sorry.'

'Where are they?'

Sally says go to the Brotherhood retreat and collect Shannon's kids. Callum and Susan took them from school when Hamilton was rushed to hospital. Shannon wants space to think and reconsider her marriage, take advice from her family and friends and business associates. Sally gives him a postcode. Says she'll meet him there and then straight across the Irish sea to Dublin.

'Who is paying for all this?'

'Good deeds PLC...you and me.'

'He's loaded.'

'Shannon has no access to money. You want her to sign an IOU?'

'No,' says Mike, embarrassed at his morality slip.

Fully briefed, Mike makes a few phone calls, calls in a few favours and within a couple of hours is on the road to the Emerald Isle in a borrowed Spittal Rangers AFC branded minibus that is no longer needed as the football club folded a few years back. Like much of Berwick, the vehicle is a little worse for wear and tear.

There is a small diversion first to pick up his passengers. He drives the red and blue minibus into the court yard of a very spacious country manor with swimming pool, tennis courts, stables and extensive manicured gardens with its own shooting range and fishing lake. Signage around the site underplays the Brotherhood of Jesus brand in favour of the Pentland Valley Estate. According to the main entrance sign, Pentland Valley is a large, rural, agricultural estate waiting to be explored and discovered. Lying in the valley of the River Tweed in the northernmost corner of Northumberland, within a stone's throw of the Scottish Border and the beautiful Northumbrian coastline. Mike would be impressed if he aspired to that rich man's lifestyle. Whatever was available here, could also be found in Berwick and the surrounding countryside and coastlines free of charge.

Mike's greeted by Callum Petty, dressed as a country squire without any crosses to bear around his neck.

'What are you doing here? This place is out of your price range, my friend. You've not come back for round two?' smiles Callum.

'Do you own all this?'

'Not me, the Brotherhood.'

'Who owns the Brotherhood?'

'God.'

'And?'

'Jesus. You're very tedious. The Brotherhood is more than happy to help Robin recuperate and rehabilitate from his surgery. We're all touched by your presence, dear chap, but I hope this a fleeting visit.'

'I've come for Shannon and her kids.'

'So they tell me. Whenever there is a nasty smell, you're never far away.'

Mike shrugs and asks where the girls are.

'Wait here, my friend.'

Callum disappears into the mansion and Mike looks around and thinks the whole estate is an accident waiting to happen. Charlie Cortez would have a field day boobytrapping the estate.

As Callum walks in through the tall mansion double-doors, Sally walks out, still in her uniform, also looking a little weary, a little worse for wear and tear.

'Lucy's inside, flapping around. Her intern is with Robin at the hospital. Lucy is trying to reach a deal with Shannon,' says Sally.

'Will she win her over?'

'We'll find out if she comes out with the kids and her bags.'

'She's going to go back to him, isn't she?'

'He holds all the cards and has enough juice to make her life very difficult.'

'Are we wasting our time?'

'Save one person, you save the world.'

'Did you read that on a mug?'

'White tee-shirt.'

They smile at each other and share the moment.

'Do you feel her with us?'

'All the time.'

They give themselves a minute or two. Lucy must be a persuasive woman, almost at the top of her profession, listing England's most famous living satirist amongst her clients.

Sally breaks the silence and asks Mike for more details about his showdown with Simon Lord. What exactly, if anything, did he cough.

'Our list of prime suspects is diminishing all the time. We have three options. The Brays. The Pettys. Or Lisa herself.'

'Or me,' says Sally. 'How come he played ball so quickly.'

'Charlie Cortez.'

'Charlie Cortez. I was beginning to think your so-called friend sounds as made up as Hamilton's J.D. Hammerhead.'

'He's made up. Do you think we'll be using his real name and presenting our heads on a plate to the police and the CPS? If you wanna find the real Charlie you're gonna have to check every single person I've served with over the years which is probably thousands of Marines and try and spot who might be my special buddy. Be like trying to find a needle in a haystack, but good luck. Charlie's surname is taken from the Neil Young song about *Cortez the Killer* and Charlie from The Clash song about surfing. Our little private joke we developed in war zones. Anyone to blame for a death, we'd name Charlie Cortez. *Hey, is Charlie being a naughty boy again.*'

'I googled Gannon. A gruesome death,' says Sally.

'Gannon was bad mouthing me every chance he got, protecting his own tattered reputation. In the aftermath of my accident, word got around he was not reliable, and his work dried up. He had to lower his rates and his ambitions. He went from a stunt co-ordinator to a stunt runner, fetch this, fetch that. Give him a drink and he would soon be trashing my name. He didn't know when to keep his mouth zipped.'

'Did you...'

'I've not been back to the US since my accident. Not left England up until today. Here, check my passport.'

'You're cool. We know the approximate truth. The guilty are being punished in hell. This short little road trip will be our long goodbye.'

'No more flirting?'

'I am married. Me and Ian had a long chat last night about where our marriage is going and we decided it is time to start a family or have fun trying. We are going to find time to make more love without any pressure on him to perform. He's been reading about tantric sex.'

'Good for him. That's a big about turn?'

'Sorry. Did you have great expectations for me?'

I have no expectations of anyone or anything. Without believing in God, I have no expectations of passing through here again. Life is random and you took whatever it threw at you with a pinch of salt. If you took it too seriously, you were well and truly fucked and would end up disappointed at the final accounting. You did what you did and lived with the consequences. Lisa understood it. We had clicked the moment we met, just got each other big time. That doesn't happen often. Once is more than enough. I wasn't wood and she wasn't wood either. Our sapling would have been loved, not lost.

The front doors to the mansion open again and Shannon stands there with her three children, waving over to Mike and Sally. She is shouting, let's go.

Three hours later Mike's playing airline pilots with the children, pretending they are flying in a Jumbo jet on a huge adventure into the unknown. He weaves stories around things they see as they pass. He has one ear on the kids' gleeful responses and half an ear on the conversation going on behind him.

Shannon talks to Sally about her so-called literary career. If she was being one hundred percent honest, it wasn't her poetry. She'd start something with an idea and Robin would finish and polish her poems, give them a literary glaze good enough to fool the critics. Only him, her and Lucy know the truth. He has a gift for words. They come easy to him. Lucy says her career is over if he won't help her finish her verses and Shannon says she doesn't mind; a girl must stand on her own two feet sooner or later. She's confident she can write poetry without his input.

Shannon briefly discusses the book out of earshot of the kids when they are crossing the Irish Sea. Shannon says that the book was pure filth, and she told him to stop writing them, but he carried on because they made so much money. She doesn't know where he got the information from and just assumes it was his filthy dirty imagination. She said it was impossible to lie next to somebody with so much filth rotting in their heads and it made her feel filthy and unclean and unwashed. Not just her husband, Callum Petty and Bryan Bray were constants throughout their marriage. They were like public schoolboys who never grew up, mummy's boys who never cut the apron strings, giggling at their secret language, laughing when Robin would assault Shannon sexually at public gatherings.

They drop off Shannon and her kids in a small seaside town outside Dublin. Her parents and two brothers greet them when they arrive and insist on giving them a meal before their return to Holyhead. Mike gets on with Shannon's men, bonding over football, boxing and music and steering clear of the Troubles.

On the way back, Sally drives and Mike kips and then she kips, and he drives. There isn't much time for talking.

They are back in Berwick in the early hours, the dawn already rising and Mike says does she want breakfast and a coffee and a proper sleep before her journey south. They've been on a long journey together that's coming to an end and the time has come to say goodbye rather than make futile promises to stay in touch. Only Lisa and a shared sardonic black humour unite them. There's not enough there to change the world and create a new universe for themselves.

'Do you want Lisa's violas? They are in my sister's bedroom. The Pettys have never mentioned them. You could play them or give them to young musicians who cannot afford quality instruments.'

'Sure, would be an honour.'

I don't know why I never tell strangers about my sister. Maybe I don't want their pity, or I like the thought of Angelina having an alternative life where she is happy, working in London and living the life with a family and children, his nephews, and not in a permanent vegetative state. I told Lisa, but not Sally. Maybe, that's the difference between love and friendship, the confidences you share.

They messed my sister up, individuals and cash-strapped systems conspired to fuck her life up. Too many opportunities were missed and despite access to medical care and medical professionals, an overdose saw her brain starved of oxygen and left her unable to do anything for herself. She'd been out of it for 10 years and I had introduced her to Lisa to try and explain to her exactly what the consequences of a failed suicide look like. Nobody understands what is going on inside her head and it really was just a matter of waiting. The doctors said she might just snap out of it one day and that'll be it. She'll be back amongst the living. She might have to learn to do everything, but they just don't know, there is no science behind it. No logic. One day the lights might just switch on. Will she remember our coma conversations? I hope not. I'll have a lot of explaining to do.

Inside Angelina's bedroom, Mike unlocks a cupboard, and he opens what is left of Lisa's world. He explains she travelled lightly when she was in Berwick, lived out of a couple of back packs. All her music, books and movies were stored on her iPad and mobile phone. They had been surrendered to the police and WPC Chandler had passed them onto her family.

I open one of her viola cases, my eyes ignore the instrument Lisa played so beautifully and practised so assiduously. They are immediately drawn to dozens of polaroid images kept together with a couple of rubber bands. Slowly, I pull them off and start to flick through the images, like I am picking through a card deck, looking for the jokers in the pack. In my hands is Lisa's precious life story captured in snapshots of time on her own polaroid camera. Forty key moments that define her as a young religious child, a musical schoolgirl and a professional violist; selfies taken before that became a thing. Lots of her and Sally together, soul mates across the years, always happy, playing music, eating, shopping, nights out. Another selfie, four in a hotel room. Sally's in a black zip-up dress with men with moustaches. And then there's me near the end of the pack. On the doorstep that first time and in bed with her and her smile. She must have stolen it back. Me sleeping, her head on my scars, stoking me. It gets sinister towards the end. Her aged 14, topless by herself and then with the Brays, all three of them in various states of undress. I force myself to carry on looking at the final polaroid. A man and woman lying bloody and bruised in a car, airbags inflated, heads resting against them like they were pillows. Bryan and Betty Bray dead in Italy, now waiting on the imminent return of Jesus Christ so they can be resurrected. Fat chance.

'What is this?'

Mike hands the image of the dead Brays to Sally.

'Don't know,' she says.

Sally studies it and hands it back to Mike.

'Presumably Lisa took it?'

'I don't know.'

Mike notices two sealed envelopes tucked away in the case. He pulls them out to read. There is no need to worry about Lisa's privacy now. It's all a bit late.

He scans the notes and hands them to Sally. Her testimony at the inquest exonerated, but he always knew she was telling the truth.

Bryan Bray (aged age 43), Betty Bray (aged 39) and Lisa Petty (aged 14) pledge the following indefinite commitments to each other.

We, Bryan Bray and Betty Bray, on the 21 June 2005, promise we will do everything in our power to ensure:-

1.   Lisa Petty graduates with distinction from the Great Northern College off Music and Performing Arts

2.   Lisa Petty has a successful and lucrative professional music career with the prestigious musical organisation, at a minimum, is contracted to the Great Northern Philharmonic Orchestra

3.   Lisa Petty is given two suitable violas for a topclass violist.

4.   Sally Bond also graduates and has the same opportunities as

Lisa Petty to work with professional orchestras and under no circumstances will she be forced to leave the college prematurely for any reason.

The Brays also pledge that the relationship between them is exclusive, and they will not touch any other pupils, students or young people in or outside of the Great Northern College of Music and Performing Arts.

In return, Lisa Petty promises to provide her body, but not her mind or her soul, for the sexual amusement and pleasure of Bryan and Betty Bray, excluding male penetrative sexual intercourse. The safe word — Shostakovich — will be adhered to the moment it is uttered, no matter what is happening.

Lastly, but not least, Bryan and Betty Bray swear to their GOD that they will never ever talk about this agreement or our sexual relationship under any circumstances whatsoever to anyone or the nature of Lisa Petty's compliance. The severity of the punishment for breaking this pledge in anyway, no matter how small or trivial, will be decided by Lisa Petty.

Signed
Bryan   *Betty*   *Lisa*

'Did you know these agreements existed?'

'No.'

'Honestly?'

'I'd have given them to the police.'

'Would you? They would have convicted the Brays if they hadn't had the misfortune to die before their peers held them to account. That was a lucky break.'

The second non-disclosure-agreement was signed on the date Lisa Petty graduated from the Great Northern College of Music and Performing Arts; similar to the first signed four years earlier. This was more condensed and to the point.

Bryan Bray (aged 47), Betty Bray (aged 43) and Lisa Petty (aged 18, now known as Lisa Wright) confirm:-

- *Their previous sexual pleasure agreement is now null and void and there is no more sexual relationship.*
- *Lisa is entitled to keep the two violas provided by the Brays for her services.*
- *The Brays swear not to sexually assault or have consensual sex with Lisa's fellow pupils.*
- *The Brays and Lisa also commit 100% to never, ever discuss the sexual relationship between them and Lisa Petty (now known as Lisa Wright) in any shape or form with anyone ever.*

If this clause is broken, Lisa Petty (now known as Wright) can impose a suitable punishment at her sole discretion.

Signed
Bryan   *Betty*   *Lisa*

Both handwritten documents are signed and dated by all three participants. The writing on the first NDA was childlike, letters scribbled without following any discernible style or pattern. The second one was much more mature and controlled lettering, almost like print. The discipline that she had shown with her music also applied to the written word in black ink.

Was that what living in a religious cult made you, cold and emotionless? Was this definitive proof that Lisa was complicit and manipulative, benefiting from selling her body to the Brays for sex at the age of 14? No, it was never her fault. All she was doing was copying what she had seen Callum and Susan do, write pledges and then do whatever they wanted to do in the first place. Their religion was a mask, a disguise of their post-truth dishonesty, their only goal was whether their actions were advantageous or disadvantageous to them at any point in time. It's a pure, naked transaction and that's how Lisa thought she should behave as a normal human being. Was this the reason for her silence? She believed the pledge was worth keeping, the key to incessant abuse? They left her with no choice. She was bound by the pledges as much as they should have been. Everything made sense and nothing did anymore. Poor confused Lisa.

Mike holds Lisa's polaroids and sex pledges in his hand. There are numerous other notes and agreements too.

On his own phone he has pictures of Stevie Gannon sliced into four pieces of human shit. Artificial intelligence, a mate who lives down Mexico way. Emile Perez now works in animation. Told Mike about Gannon topping himself when his work dried up. The two images...a shared joke between two Marines who respect each other. There are also images of two men, randomly attacked in pubs, mugged for phones and petty cash. One of them, called Roger, had his fingers broken in multiple places, a reminder not to poke them where they were not wanted in future.

He opens the second case. Inside is Lisa's passport and various plastic IDs, including one for the Great Northern Philharmonic Orchestra, her pride and joy.

Mike picks up the passport. Flicks it a bit. Opens it. Looks at Lisa's passport, sees her stamps from all her musical globetrotting. She must have clocked up a few air miles during her travels. At the time of the Brays' death, she was in Italy, a coincidence or...

'When did they die?' asks Mike, already knowing the answer.

Sally gives him a date.

'I am not a betting man, but I am sure you have the same Italian stamps as Lisa's in your passport. I've seen you drive. I can picture somebody forcing them off the road and over the cliffs.'

'No comment.'

'Your idea or hers?'

'You have a vivid imagination. You could never prove it.'

'Who says I want to prove it.'

'You once said nothing is ever an accident — everything happens for a reason.'

'It's true. But there is no such thing as poetic justice.'

'Nothing happened.'

'I don't care, Sally. You did what you had to do. When you kill in cold blood, a little bit of you dies too until you end up screaming at people for caring, cursing them for sharing. Was it worth it?'

'Was Gannon?'

'Now, I am going to echo you. Nothing to do with me. Charlie Cortez is all in my head. A coping mechanism to justify my bloody deeds. Another Marine joke to blame our atrocities on.'

'It is all over now for you and me... better we move on. Lisa is dead ... nothing will bring her back.'

'One more run before you go?'

15

They run fast and hard to the top of the cliffs where angels fail to fly. Near where Lisa fell, they dig a hole, start a fire and burn incriminating polaroids and damning letters pledging compliance and silence. Once they've burnt them, they refill the hole, trample it down.

'I am going to carry on my run to the railway crossing,' says Mike.

'I have to head back to work and Ian.'

'Good luck.'

'You too, Pretty Boy. In a parallel universe perhaps...'

'Lisa got there first ... if the guilt gets too much, call me.'

'I might hold you to that offer one day.'

They run off in opposite directions at pace without looking back in anger or regret.

I look at the spot where Lisa went over the edge. Had she tried to take me on the left-hand side, nearest the cliffs? I'll never know if I covered the break and cut her off or my elbow caught her, causing her to tumble to avoid getting hit in the face. There was no contact, I know that for definite, but she was much closer than I've ever told anyone. Why did I lie and suffer in silence? I live with the uncertainty daily and always will. I wake most mornings and think of us running or chilling out in my bed or hers like she never died, and we had all the time in the world to mend ourselves.

I suppose it's not knowing for sure. An accident means Lisa saw a future with me. Suicide says there was none. And that hurts, if you don't love yourself and others enough to live.

Is Sally another Lisa? She will tell me in her own good time one day, if, and when, she's ever ready and tantric sex overstays its welcome. That's all part of my unwritten future.

I live only in the present. Sometimes, when I play Shostakovich's Symphony No. 5 or Cortez the Killer on SIRI it's OK, for about forty-five minutes with the Great Northern Philharmonic Orchestra and six with Mr Neil Young. I am closest to Lisa then, feel her spirit embracing me, like the cold breezes blowing hard across the North Sea, and, of course, when I run, she's always by my side with our child. Running free, spurring me on...

'THOSE WHO HAVE EARS TO HEAR, WILL HEAR.'
DMITRI SHOSTAKOVICH

Also by Hit the North
www.hitthenorth.co.uk

After the Bridge by Andrew J Field

Two suicidal strangers, failing actor Owen and traumatised Ukrainian refugee Becky, postpone death on the Humber bridge to honey-trap married men. They make easy money until they reach Manchester when a corrupt civil servant dies on Becky in a hotel room. Owen steals the dead man's identity to con a small fortune from a brain-damaged hero's trust fund. His impersonation is good, but doesn't fool a cynical cop or the deceased's self-harming granddaughter. As their blackmail scam spirals out of control, Owen and Becky must confront their own personal demons or risk drowning in a sea of corruption and criminality.

All Down the Line by Andrew J Field

Manchester 2017: Cain Bell thinks he has finally found happiness with April Sands, a celebrated chef and the love of his life. But on the night he proposes, April reveals a shocking secret: the man who confessed to killing Cain's daughter in a hit-and-run accident two decades ago was not the real driver. As Cain seeks answers, he discovers April harbours many more dark secrets — one of them ties her to the very tragedy that has haunted him for years. Caught between seeking vengeance and turning the other cheek, Cain must navigate the blurred lines between right and wrong in pursuit of a truth that will either renew or destroy him.

Without Rules by Andrew J Field

China is fighting back against her abusers. She knows she must win, whatever the cost, otherwise she is mincemeat. Sexually abused as a young teen, China fears her young daughter is next the gang's next victim unless she can finally permanently break free from her abusers.

But she can only do this if she is more ruthless than her evil amoral abusers. When her initial plan ends up in a bloodbath, she must team up a cold-blooded killer suffering from PTSD and forget all the rules if she and her daughter are to survive the wicked games of evil men.

ALWAYS ADAM BY MARK BRUMBY

London-based financial journalist Spencer Beck is obsessed with billionaire biotech prodigy, Adam Reid, orphaned in his mid-teens when his parents died in a tragic murder-suicide in New York City. A shadowy informant with MI5 connections promises Beck unfettered access to the mysterious Reid and introduces him to Daniel Flanagan, a retired Big Apple detective who investigated the deaths of Adam's mother and father. Spencer's initial scepticism, fed by the suspicions of the former police officer, turns to excitement when Reid reveals the truth about himself and his altruistic ambitions to protect society from a deadly virus with a powerful vaccine he's developed. But when Beck's entire world starts to implode, he discovers Reid harbours a vendetta that, left unchecked, threatens not only his survival but that of an entire species.

BIG DADDY BY MARK BRUMBY

Vikings wake in the tenth century and die in the twentieth. A Nazi platoon massacres civilians in Poland fifty years after Adolf Hitler's death. A B-29 bomber, lost in 1945, resumes a mission in 1999 to drop an atomic bomb on Tokyo. Big Daddy is larger than the Little Boy and Fat Man bombs that devastated Hiroshima and Nagasaki respectively. Now, at the turn of the 21st century, world leaders and scientists race against time to locate and neutralise the scientist behind a timeless flight where the future of humanity is hanging in the balance. Mark Brumby's Big Daddy is a masterful story packed full of suspense, science fiction ingenuity and historical intrigue.